A BIT OF HEAVEN ON EARTH

ALEXA ASTON

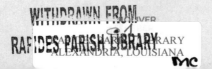

PROLOGUE
ENGLAND—1347

Lady Elizabeth Bramwell of Aldwyn plopped upon the hearth, stretching out her long legs as she carefully concealed the breeches she wore under her borrowed kirtle. She yawned wearily, tired from her day of riding and exploring. The fire warmed her back and would hopefully dry her auburn hair, heavy from the summer shower she'd been caught in that afternoon. She ran a hand through her thick mass of curls, using her fingers to pull any knots free.

"I will have *no more* of this, Elizabeth," her father roared. "You ignore me at your peril."

She steeled herself for their usual argument. "Then quit parading suitors before me." She tossed her head, the wild auburn curls spilling about her shoulders. "'Tis a waste of their time and yours, not to mention mine."

She ignored his murderous glare and continued slipping her fingers through her tangled locks, hoping a servant would interrupt her father with a situation that needed his immediate attention. If so, she could slip away from the great hall and avoid this entire conversation.

Unfortunately, that didn't happen. Instead, her father began pacing the room, his voice bellowing as she imagined it did on the battlefield when he shouted orders to his loyal knights. She thought it loud enough that possible King Edward in London might be able to hear of her wrongdoing.

Her red-faced parent paused in front of her. "You think you can control your hair? I would but wish I could tame those devilish red locks. 'Twould be a start to taming *you*."

"My hair has as much brown as red in it, Father."

He threw his hands up in despair. "That's not the point, Elizabeth. I swear it's the Devil Himself in you causing you to act the way you do."

Though she knew where the conversation headed, she couldn't help her retort. "And besides my shade of hair, what fault do you find with my behavior?"

Her father fisted his hands at his sides and took a deep breath. "You cannot run off every time I summon an eligible man to Aldwyn, Daughter."

"Why not?"

Her father began harping again, his long strides carrying him back and forth across the great hall. Elizabeth tuned out his lengthy tirade. After ten-and-seven years, she knew her list of transgressions by heart and could recite them from memory. On any given day, her father's litany of his only child's misconduct might go on for hours. It usually began with the fact that she was too headstrong. Unmanageable. Stubborn. Willful.

Then he'd move on and claim that she'd run wild, as if she were some hound that should be bent to a strong master's will. Her father always managed to point out that no suitor pleased her. Ever. Elizabeth took secret pride in the fact that two had even asked to be released from their intended betrothal to her because of her strong will.

But his next words did not fall on deaf ears.

"... so in that case I have no choice, Daughter. I will force you into a convent and wash my hands of you."

She smiled sweetly, ready to meet any challenge he threw her way.

"Then I shall merely plot my escape. Run away." She placed her elbows upon her knees, resting her chin upon her fists. "Admit it, Father. I am incorrigible. You cannot make me do anything, especially find a convent that would want me. I would surmise that within a week the good nuns and their mother abbess would push me outside and lock the gates to keep me from returning to their fold."

She stood and dusted the front of her man's dark brown tunic, one she had swiped from where it lay drying in the sun. She left a gold coin in its place, knowing the owner would come out the better in the trade.

Her father looked at her solemnly. "Just as I thought you would say. Which is why I now produce this."

Elizabeth watched warily as he walked to an oak chest and lifted its lid. He removed a thick scroll. She knew exactly what that meant.

"Sweet Jesu, Father. Not another betrothal contract?"

"Hush," he commanded. "This time you'll see a marriage through. 'Tis to a much older man. He will settle you down. He has had two previous wives and already has three children by them, though the eldest died last year in the French wars. He will know how to discipline such wayward behavior. Hopefully, he'll get you with child and keep you that way for the next dozen years or more. Lots of babes will take all these wild notions from your head."

"Wild notions? Simply because I refuse to behave like a simpering—"

"Watch what you say, Elizabeth. Do not tread lightly on Thera's memory."

She frowned. "I do not tread upon my mother's memory. I have no memory of her. How can I blacken what I have no knowledge of?"

But Elizabeth did know. Lady Thera, from the descriptions she gleaned from servants over the years, had been full of sweetness and light, attending to her husband's every whim. From an early age, Elizabeth knew she would never live up to what her gentle mother had been, so why begin to try?

Instead, she'd become the exact opposite. She was unladylike, volatile, and had a stubborn streak combined with a will of iron. She believed she would have made an excellent commander on the battlefield. Quick-witted and able to size up people in a matter of seconds, she'd been at war with her father for her entire life.

Usually on the winning side.

Why would she wish to have another, older man aim to tame her, breaking her spirit like that of a lively horse? No, thank you. Elizabeth was happy having already bent her father to her will. At least most of the time. He would get over this latest idea of fancy. Eventually, she would make him see that marriage was not a part of what she wanted.

"Bloody hell," Elizabeth swore softly under her breath.

Now married, she sat at the head table in her wedding finery. Her father must have planned this marriage for quite some time, for her cotehardie and sideless surcoat had been made from the finest of silks. The rich scarlet and gold of both had delicate embroidery, so intricate she knew that a skilled seamstress had labored many months over its completion. Even her jeweled belt could be seen as a work of art, its golden chains embellished with rubies and freshwater pearls. No expense had been spared for this wedding attire. She viewed it and her generous dowry as a bribe from her father to her new husband. Lord Bramwell of Aldwyn had dressed up his daughter as a rare prize, but he was more than happy another man now took her off his hands. With the distance between Aldwyn and Kentwood, she doubted after today that she would ever see her father again.

The interminable feast progressed as slowly as the labor of a woman's first babe. She'd lost count of the number of courses served over the last few hours. Duck, venison, roasted pig and goose, stewed apples and plums, cheeses, and cakes abounded.

Many were her favorite foods. She supposed her father had passed word along to the Kentwood kitchens, trying to appease her in no small way. She did love to eat. But not today.

Her wedding day.

She glanced from the corner of her eye to the old nobleman seated next to her. *Her husband.* He was well over six feet, with broad shoulders and a thatch of thick, white hair to match his equally white beard. She couldn't place his age although she'd recognized his name the moment she heard it.

Aldred.

Lord Aldred of Kentwood. A legend throughout England for his warrior's skills and cunning. Troubadours sang of his valor and victories as if he were a god. She doubted if there were a single person in all of England who hadn't heard of Lord Aldred's prowess on the battlefield.

Yet this gallant soldier, a favorite of King Edward, must be at least three score, mayhap more. Her groom, who used a walking stick to lean upon as he got around, was much older than any suitor her father presented in the past, and it worried her beyond measure.

Elizabeth wished both Lord Aldred and her father would fall over dead on the spot. She wondered idly if she would be entitled to any of Kentwood's wealth if that small miracle occurred in the next few minutes.

Her father had outsmarted her, after all. Instead of the wedding party arriving at Aldwyn and the marriage taking place from the bride's home, her father had brought her to Kentwood and this elderly bridegroom, with the help of Aldwyn's healer. Elizabeth would love to know what had been placed in her drink at the evening meal. She had lost two full days' time after consuming it.

She awakened miles away from home with heavy limbs and a throbbing headache. What little she'd seen of the property from her window was impressive, she admitted to herself, but she did not want to be at Kentwood. Did not want to be married to an old goat. Couldn't begin to imagine what awaited her upstairs in the marriage bed.

She shuddered and reached for her goblet. Mayhap the wine would dull her senses. If she drank enough of it, hopefully she would have no recollection of what would take place this night.

Suddenly, a hand rested upon her wrist. "I would guess you have had enough, my dear."

Elizabeth finally looked into the eyes of her new husband for the first time. Aldred. His voice was gentle, but the stern look he gave her was enough to make her set down the golden cup. She bit her lip in frustration. This was going to be far more challenging than she'd thought. Lord Aldred might be advanced in years, but steely resolve ran through him. She was certain of it.

"I think we've both had enough of the merriment, don't you agree, my lady?"

For a moment, she detected a mischievous glint in his eyes, then it was gone. Had it been a mere shadow? She gripped her hands tightly in her lap.

Lowering her eyes demurely, she said, "Whatever you say, my lord."

Her new husband chuckled. "You need not be meek with me, Elizabeth. I know a strong-willed woman when I see one. I have even heard a few tales about you. Quite interesting ones indeed."

She looked up at him quickly. "What tales?" She studied him carefully. "Mayhap you are not as wise as I was led to believe, my lord, if you heard such tales and still chose to wed me."

He suppressed a smile. "Oh, I believe I know exactly what I have gotten myself into, wife of mine." He rose and offered her his hand. "Come."

They made their way through the great hall, drunken revelers shouting their good wishes to them. Elizabeth met her father's eyes defiantly before turning and ascending the stairs with her husband.

Her husband.

Her stomach lurched, bringing a wave of nausea. God in Heaven, what would come next? Actually, she had more than an inkling of what would be expected of her. When a child, she'd stumbled upon couples on three separate occasions in the stables, naked as newborns, caught up in their lovemaking. She'd thought the act disgusting. Besides, she knew it must be quite hurtful, as both the men and women cried out and quivered and moaned as if in great agony.

She'd also seen babes born on a few occasions. If that kind of pain were the result of a quick coupling, she decided long ago to have none of it. Her own mother had died in childbirth when Elizabeth was but two. The babe that came from Lady Thea lived only a few hours. Why would women put themselves through something of that nature?

No, Elizabeth decided long ago that physical love was not for her. She'd had no mother to correct her assumptions. She liked her life exactly the way it had been. Why ruin it? She didn't need or want love. Instead, she desired more than anything to learn. To travel. A thousand experiences would be more gratifying than the act of love.

Yet here she was, ready to do the very thing she found loathsome, legally bound to a man whom she knew nothing about, other than what she had heard praised in song. Nothing she could do or say would prevent her new husband from exercising his rights by law. Any independence she'd once possessed ended with the vows she had uttered under duress in front of dozens of witnesses. She was little more than chattel to Lord Aldred of Kentwood, and beyond the ample dowry her father had provided, Elizabeth had no value to this man.

Aldred led her down a large hallway lined in stone

and lit by sconces. Her heart pounded with each step she made, the sound echoing in her ears. They reached the solar all too quickly, and Lord Aldred opened the heavy wooden door and motioned her inside. She quickly took in that her personal possessions had been transferred from her guest bedchamber while she had been at the ceremony and subsequent feast. Her brush lay on a table by the bed. Her blue bed robe had been draped across a chair.

Elizabeth's belly rebelled at the thought of sharing intimate details of her life with anyone, much less losing all privacy to a stranger—especially one who would force her into all kinds of vile acts. She knew from experience, though, to show no weakness, whether to friend or foe. She sucked in a quick breath and then exhaled slowly, hoping it would calm her.

She held her head high. She would dance to Lord Aldred's tune in the bedroom if she must, but she refused to lose herself. She could learn to control this new husband of hers, learn to placate him, even live a separate life from him. She'd heard many couples did just that. Beyond the bedroom, they rarely even spoke. She hoped Lord Aldred would subscribe to this kind of marriage. She doubted she could tolerate more.

"Have a seat, Elizabeth. Let us talk and get to know one another a bit. We have not been given time to do so, in part due to the haste in which Fayne insisted that our marriage take place." A shadow crossed his face. "I am sorry for the way you were brought here. 'Twas not my wish to see you come to Kentwood in such a manner."

He gave her a small smile. "Please. Come and sit. I would take care to know my new wife."

Though her legs were a bit wobbly, she managed

to glide to the proffered seat as if being alone with a strange, old man was the most natural thing in the world. Lord Aldred took the seat opposite her, slipping off his boots and propping his crossed feet upon the hearth in order to warm his feet.

"What a good idea," she proclaimed, and she did likewise. He looked shocked at first and then laughed heartily with approval.

"Your father said you were... high-spirited." His eyes glowed with unspoken approval. "I think we will do quite well together, my dear. Let us speak frankly and learn about one another."

He poured wine for them both, and Elizabeth let him talk on a bit as she sipped the sweetened liquid. Lord Aldred explained that he'd been married twice before. She had met his two children earlier at the marriage feast, a son who was a sturdy lad, tall and outgoing, and a shy wisp of a daughter with raven hair. The long day was such a blur she couldn't even recall their names now. As he spoke, she gradually began to relax a little. He seemed a decent sort. Mayhap this act of love could happen quickly and be done with.

Lord Aldred reached out and took her hand in his gnarled one. "I made both my wives happy, Elizabeth. I hope I can make you so."

Her stomach knotted as the old warrior stood and gently pulled her to her feet. He kissed her forehead with surprising tenderness and led her to the curtained bed.

"I know this is awkward, my dear. I shall leave you to prepare. I will return in—"

"No," Elizabeth interjected. If he left, her fears would grow. She might even try to slip out of the castle. She wouldn't cause him the embarrassment of having to track down a runaway bride in front of all his guests, not when he'd already tried so hard to be kind to her.

"I am ready to do my duty now, Husband. Simply tell me what you expect of me. I had no mother to train me. I fear I am ill-prepared in this venture."

He studied her. The flickering shadows from the candles played across his lined face. She locked her knees together and stood her ground. She took a deep breath and steadied herself.

"I see," he said after a long moment. "Loosen your hair, then pull back the bed curtains and climb upon the bed. I will do my best in initiating you into the mysteries of marriage." He touched her cheek and stroked it. "Do not fear me, Elizabeth. You have great spirit. I would not see that change."

His words brought her some comfort. She did as he instructed, pulling the caul from her head and un-binding her mass of curls. She pushed away the cur-tains and thought she should at least remove her surcoat and cote-hardie. Without turning, she word-lessly slipped out of them and tossed the garments aside, though she wouldn't part with her kirtle. The thought of his old, weathered hands touching her bare skin caused her to tremble. She eased upon the raised bed and settled onto her back. Her heart raced. Her limbs felt stiff and heavy.

Despite the amount of wine she'd drunk, she found her mouth had gone dry. She bit her lip again as Lord Aldred went about the room, extinguishing candles, leaving the fire as the only light in the room. As he began to disrobe, she closed her eyes. She swal-lowed hard as he joined her upon the bed, drawing the curtains.

Aldred talked to her softly, murmuring words of

comfort as he explained what they both would do. Elizabeth nodded, her voice failing her. She could do this. She would do this.

It didn't go as he said it would. Oh, he touched her face and kissed her gently, caressed his hands up and down her body, cupped her breasts as she lay there, wishing herself far away. Yet when it came time for him to enter her, something was wrong.

Fearing his wrath, she said meekly, "I am sorry, my lord. Perhaps I did not quite understand what I am to do. This doesn't seem to be going according to your plan."

Her husband sighed and rolled from atop her, coming to rest beside her. He stared blankly up at the ceiling. Elizabeth lay motionless. Then her natural curiosity could stand no more. She turned to her side, propping her head upon her elbow.

"What am I doing wrong, my lord? If you will but explain things again, 'tis certain I will get it right this time. I have always been a quick learner. I do not wish to disappoint you in any way."

Her husband's head turned. His eyes took her in. Elizabeth saw a trace of a smile play about his thin lips.

He reached out and touched her hair, smoothing it. The gesture comforted her. "'Tis nothing you've done wrong, child. I fear despite my best plans that I cannot make love to you."

She was puzzled. "Why not? You are the one that knows how. You have done this many times in the past. If we are to accomplish this deed, then I must follow your lead. Of course, once I have mastered the task, I'd be happy to take the lead upon occasion."

His laugh was rich and deep. His thumb brushed against her cheek tenderly. "Ah, my sweet wife. My very own Elizabeth." He sighed. "'Tis an apology I must make to you."

He cupped her cheek in one hand. "I am old, my dear. And when men reach my age, many times they cannot perform the marital act. It becomes physically impossible. I thought a young, beautiful girl would make a difference. Now, in my folly, I see that it does not."

Elizabeth tried to hide her growing excitement. She wouldn't have to couple with him, after all. She sought to reassure Lord Aldred, for whom she already felt a strong fondness. "'Tis all right, my husband. If we cannot do this thing, then so be it. My loyalty remains with you."

He shook his head.

"No, 'twould not be fair to you, child. You are young and have a lifetime ahead of you. 'Twill be babes you'll soon want. A man's love that you'll need."

He sat up. "I shall see that our marriage is annulled. 'Twill free you for another, one closer to your own age."

"No," she said firmly. She pushed up until she was in a sitting position and took his rough hand in hers, holding it tightly. "I refuse to see you humiliated in such a way, my lord. I swore before God and guests to this marriage, and 'twill be so."

Aldred squeezed her fingers. "No. I cannot ask this of you, Elizabeth. I have already been fool enough."

She smiled shyly. This new husband of hers was considerate and not quite the monster she'd conjured in her mind. He seemed most reasonable. Mayhap she could strike a bargain with him.

"Actually, my lord, 'twould be you doing me the favor. You already have children and a son as your heir. I can be a mother to them. As you said, we seem to suit. I would prefer to stay and learn from you."

A look of puzzlement crossed his face. "Learn from me?"

"Yes."

Elizabeth looked at him in earnest. This would be her chance to escape her father's constant nagging. She could not return to her childhood home, especially since she knew better than to trust her father. She refused to be forced to marry against her will, especially a man that might not be as reasonable as Lord Aldred was proving to be.

"I can read and write a little. Would you be willing to teach me more, about all manner of things? Help me learn all about Kentwood and how to run a household? Allow me to be independent? I would answer to no man but you alone."

Her new husband eyed her with interest and then shook his head sadly. "It would not be fair to you."

She smiled sweetly at him. Often, her smile convinced her father when nothing else could. "In exchange, I will show you the utmost respect and affection, both in private and before the world. I shall never share what has passed between us here within the privacy of our solar."

He sized her up. "You drive a hard bargain, my lady. You truly would stay with an old man until my time is up?"

Elizabeth took both his hands in hers, eager for him to agree to her proposal. "'Tis my fondest wish, my lord. I promise to be with you always, caring for you, even until the end."

He laughed aloud, the sound of his mirth like sweet music to her ears. "I suppose 'tis not every day a man of my age gets such a magnanimous offer." He tenderly kissed her cheek. "You have your bargain, my lady. I will hold you to it. I will be your teacher and your closest friend. I will cherish you until my dying day and do whatever I can to please you in every way."

He lay back upon the pillow, pulling her down to rest next to him. "Let's get some rest, Wife," he whispered softly.

Elizabeth lay next to him, awake for some hours, while Lord Aldred snored softly. It made her slightly uncomfortable being so close to him, but he was clean, had most of his teeth, and she knew he would never mistreat her. She finally fell asleep, dreaming about all the things she would do—the books she would read in his library, helping him run his estate, mayhap even learning swordplay. Excitement filled her at such prospects.

And if she had to mother his children from another wife, so be it. How difficult could that be?

1

ASHGROVE—THE NORTH OF ENGLAND—1355

Gillian groaned as pain racked her body yet again. Cold sweat drenched her hair and the very bedclothes. She wanted it to be over. Twinges and tingles had turned from dull aches over the past months to this jarring pain, something far worse than childbirth all those years ago.

She smiled, thinking of Gavin, and wished he could be here at the end to hold her hand. The thought of her brave, handsome son brought the only comfort she'd known in days. With his image, though, guilt flooded her, as strong as any of the suffering that flowed through her now.

"What might I do to comfort you, my lady?"

She despaired as Father Michael, the doddering priest who barely knew his own name nowadays, leaned over her solicitously.

"You cannot give me physical solace, Father, but you can let me go to God with a clear conscience."

The priest looked confused. "My lady, you have always been most pious in your devotions. I have often thought a cloistered life would have suited you well."

Gillian sucked in her breath as another shot of

agony, hot as liquid fire, poured through her withered body. God punished her now for the sins of her youth. She had spent a lifetime trying to make it up to Him. Apparently, her devotion hadn't been enough to please Him. Mayhap her final words would.

"'Tis time, Father, for my last confession," she managed to say. "Then the last rites."

Suddenly, her husband stormed in. Berwyn was the last person she cared to see at her dying moment. She closed her eyes, willing him to go away. What if her wasted body expired before she could make her peace with God?

"Out, man!" Berwyn proclaimed.

She opened her eyes to see her husband pushing their priest out the bedchamber's door. If she were destined to rot in Hell, she was certain Berwyn would be there to keep her company.

"Can you not get this over with, Wife?" he demanded, not bothering to chastise her in quiet tones. "How long does it take a devout woman to die? Surely God is anxious for you to come to Him."

He narrowed his eyes and studied her, his thick lips curling in contempt. "You spent more time in conversation with God than you ever did in our marriage bed or even caring for this household. You already have one foot in the next world. If not for Gavin, your time on earth would be worthless. Hurry up and die. I wish to marry again, a woman who shall be a true wife to me."

Gillian tried to wet her cracked lips in order to issue a quick retort but failed. Berwyn sneered at her weak effort. He left the room, brushing against the old priest who stood just outside the door.

Berwyn continued down the dimly lit passageway, barely restraining his fury. He did what his father commanded years ago and married Gillian. The old man hadn't lived a twelvemonth afterward. At least Berwyn had enjoyed the wealth Gillian's dowry brought to Ashgrove. It had allowed him to expand the estate and make numerous improvements over the years.

The worst was that Berwyn found himself saddled with what might as well have been a nun for a spouse all these years. She'd produced the required heir within the first year of their union and then promptly lost all interest in carnal things.

And he was a very carnal man.

"God's teeth!" he roared.

He'd gone into the chamber that smelled like death in order to fetch a bauble for Clarine. He'd promised her a jewel after their lovemaking last night and knew he could not go to her again unless he presented the trinket. Berwyn angrily paced down the hall again to retrieve a gem from his wife's casket. She never wore them and would probably be dead by the time he placed a necklace about Clarine's luscious throat.

Father Michael no longer stood guard outside the bedchamber. Undoubtedly, he had gone inside again to offer solace to Gillian. Berwyn pushed open the door, grimacing at the stench of stale vomit that greeted him again, once more glad he had banished his wife from the solar, having servants take her to this bedchamber.

Before he could take more than a few steps, however, he halted. Gillian's faltering words forced him to a stop.

"... and so Gavin is not Berwyn's son. In truth, Father, 'tis Lord Aldred's blood that runs through my son's veins."

Shock caused a physical reaction. Bile rose in his throat. He swallowed quickly and took two steps back so as to remain out of sight. He had fostered with Lord Aldred of Kentwood when but a youth, worshipping the man far more than his own father, who was Aldred's closest friend. Lord Aldred taught him how to ride and use a sword. How to wench and drink. Now, Berwyn learned a score-and-four later that the famed nobleman had cuckolded him?

When had it transpired?

He thought back to the earliest time in his marriage. Gillian delivered a son to him eight months after their vows. She told him many times first children came early, and he hadn't any reason to question her. Gavin had been perfect in every way.

Now, he saw in an instant how much Gavin resembled his true father. Berwyn had wondered where Gavin's height had come from and his unusual eyes. Why had he been blind to the truth all these years? Rage rushed through him.

"He might have been a score more than I, yet he was the kindest man, despite his reputation as a fierce warrior. Gavin is just like him, Father. He has Aldred's eyes and smile and his gentle disposition."

Gillian moaned softly and panted like a dog would before she continued. "I have seen Gavin nurse a mare in labor with tenderness, yet 'tis fierce and unhesitating he is with his sword. A son any mother would be proud of. I have kept my secret all these years, Father. 'Twas my sin to bear. I have suffered in silence so that my son would become lord of Ashgrove."

The priest murmured soft words of absolution,

but Berwyn blocked them out. He forced his clenched fists to open and took a calming breath. His face now a blank mask, he strode through the room and placed a hand on the clergyman's back.

"Forgive my earlier outburst, Father. I regret the harsh words I spoke to my wife. I have come to beg her forgiveness, as she is so near to death."

He gave Gillian a soft smile before looking again at the cleric. "Would you allow us some privacy?"

Father Michael turned and shuffled from the room, shaking his head as he mumbled to himself. Berwyn waited until he heard the door close before he looked at his traitorous wife.

Her beauty had faded long ago. Only her eyes burned brightly in her shriveled face. They held his, questioning, unsure why he would offer her an apology.

"You're right, my dear," he said almost tenderly. "I won't beg your pardon." Berwyn moved closer to the bed, breathing from his mouth so as to keep the scent of death from his nostrils.

He placed his hands upon her bony shoulders and gripped her tightly as he brought his face close to hers. The fear in her eyes brought a smile to his face.

"I am here to tell you one thing, Wife. *Your bastard child will never be master of Ashgrove. Never.*"

Tears sprang to her eyes as he watched the realization seep through her.

"Yes, I heard your pathetic confession." Berwyn lifted a hand from her shoulder and wound his fingers around a lock of her graying hair. "I may have been fooled for years, but no more. Gavin is as good as dead to me."

He smiled at her. "As are you."

With a swift movement, Berwyn pulled a pillow

from behind Gillian's back and pressed it to her face. She struggled briefly, but the disease that ravaged her body had robbed her of her strength. When she ceased moving, he lifted the pillow and returned it from where it came.

She lay with eyes open, full of fright. Berwyn steeled himself and brushed his palm across her face, closing her eyelids. He straightened the bedclothes and then went across the room. Opening the casket that contained all of her jewels, he pawed through the contents, choosing a circlet to place inside his tunic. Clarine's golden tresses would look lovelier than usual now.

Returning to Gillian's bed, Berwyn knelt next to it. He took one of her hands in his. Already, it was cool to his touch. He bit his tongue hard to give himself a pained look, one that he hoped would pass for sorrow, and bellowed at the top of his lungs.

"Sweet Jesu! Come quickly! My wife is dead."

2

FRANCE—1356

Sir Gavin Garwood of Ashgrove awakened quickly as always, his body instantly tense, hand upon his sword. Though it was well before daylight, today was the day he would once again follow the Black Prince into battle against the French.

At five-and-ten years, Gavin had stood as large as any grown man a decade ago, when he acted as squire to Lord Aldred, who gave him permission to ride into the skirmish that lay ahead.

"If young Edward, only a year older than you, Gavin, can lead troops into battle, I suppose the time has come for you to ride by my side."

Gavin fought valiantly that day, Lord Aldred serving as his guide. Young Prince Edward had been far outnumbered by French troops, yet the royal youth guided the English lines into holding their position on the hill and on to victory. Gavin continued the fight until Edward's army, weakened by illness, was forced into battle by a vastly superior French army. Fortunately, the English longbow had again triumphed at Crecy, bringing an English victory and allowing a return to English soil for the weary soldiers.

He had itched for war again these past ten years, when a lull in the fighting between England and France had occurred. The Great Pestilence swept across Europe, and no man was safe on the battlefield from its long arm. Gavin had left Kentwood, where he had fostered, and returned home, happy to be back at Ashgrove learning how to run a large estate, as well as keeping his father's army of knights ready to fight at a moment's notice.

Finally, his time came again with today's upcoming battle. Now officially knighted, he would once more follow the Black Prince into the fight against the French. Gone, however, was Lord Aldred, who remained at Kentwood. Age had taken its toll on the gallant warrior. Since Gavin left the nobleman's service, Lord Aldred had married for a third time, almost half a score ago. The union had produced no children.

Gavin thought it most unfortunate because Lord Aldred's elder son died in the taking of Calais several years before, while his younger son fell from his horse while hunting. Paralyzed for two years, every breath an agony, the boy succumbed to the same fever that also took his younger sister. Gavin knew of these events from missives received by his father, who also had fostered under the mighty warrior and still idolized the aging knight and lord. After the deaths of Aldred's two remaining children, no further news came.

He shook himself from the past, wondering why he always became so contemplative before battle. It pained him to think of Aldred's troubles, for he loved the old lord to his core. His own father, Berwyn, never seemed more than a distant relative. They had little in common except their connection through Gillian.

Gavin smiled at the thought of his beloved

mother. Though she spent much time in prayer, she'd never been the remote parent his father had. She lavished him with love from his earliest memories. An English victory today might mean he could return home. Her health, always delicate, caused him some concern. He prayed she was well and then rose for the day.

Dace, as usual, appeared from nowhere. The loyal squire anticipated Gavin's every thought and action. He knew the boy would make a steady soldier one day. High-spirited, with boundless enthusiasm, Dace was as much family to him as Robert, his closest friend.

"Here's a loaf of bread and a bit of ham, my lord." Dace handed over the food and removed a wineskin gripped under his arm. "Wine, too. A good soldier needs his strength to enter battle."

He smiled indulgently at his retainer and ruffled the boy's hair affectionately. "Right you are, Dace. When your time comes, you will be more than ready."

Dace's eyes gleamed at the thought of entering battle.

"And did you start the morning feast without me?"

Gavin turned and saw Robert standing there. "Good morn to you, my friend. I trust you slept well?"

Robert laughed. "Like a babe, Gavin. The thought of battle may terrify most, but somehow 'tis a sense of peace that falls over me the night before a conflict begins."

Gavin handed him the wineskin, and Robert took a swig. "Nectar from the gods. These French know how to do something right, after all."

The three chuckled, and Gavin tore a hunk of bread from his loaf and shared the rest with his trusted companions. They talked for a few minutes before Dace reminded them they must prepare themselves for the fight ahead.

As the squire dressed the two knights for battle, Gavin looked fondly upon them both. Dace he'd known since the boy was a tot, but Robert came from a manor in the south, close to Lord Aldred's estate. They'd met years ago and had renewed their friendship when Robert rushed to Gavin's aid in battle. They had fought side by side ever since. An established trust between them made Robert the brother Gavin never had. He couldn't conceive going into war without the steadfast Robert next to him.

"Ready?"

Gavin adjusted his cuirass and nodded to his friend, and then issued his usual warning to Dace to stay far back from the action. "I can care for myself and if trouble should arise, Robert will be there to aid me. You are to remain here, Dace. Understood?"

The squire nodded his head, but Gavin had his doubts whether the boy would listen this time. At four-and-ten, Dace was eager to enter battle and prove his prowess. He also had a sweetheart back home. He'd confided to Gavin that he couldn't wait to tell her tales of his bravery against the French. Knowing that, Gavin thought Dace might become a little careless, thus he always reminded him of his duties.

"Yes, my lord. Your horses are ready."

The noblemen followed Dace to their warhorses. Gavin smelled the excitement in the early morning light, hovering across the multitude of men gathered to fight. The Black Prince, heir to England's throne, inspired courage and loyalty among his men. Those present were eager to prove their worth to their royal commander, whose black armor gave him his nickname.

Robert slapped him on the back. "We have God upon our side, Gavin. The Almighty would not have given us victory at Crecy and allowed us to take Calais, nay, even control of the Channel itself, were we not on the side of right."

Gavin nodded, agreeing with Robert's words. He longed for this fight to be over, for England to take the south of France and allow the Black Prince to rule in Aquitaine. King Edward, still in good health, looked to be upon the throne in England for many years to come. 'Twould be only right for young Prince Edward to have his own place to rule, as part of English territory, and reward for the great service he'd given both his father and country in their conflict against the bastard French.

He looked about him. Archers, pikemen, light infantry, and cavalry were all in sight, as they had been years before at Crecy. This combined force had proven effective. He was surprised that the French clung to their old-fashioned ways of fighting after that humiliating defeat. He predicted a quick victory for England today.

Gavin mounted his horse. Dace handed over his sugarloaf great helm, and he slipped it onto his head. Most of the early morning light ceased, the slit only allowing in a small portion of the sun's rays. Last, Dace gave him his shield. He gripped it firmly in one hand, the reins of his warhorse in the other. He looked to Robert and nodded as they trotted their coal-black destriers forward.

Another wave of arrows whizzed over Gavin's head. Everywhere he looked in front of him, men fell left and right, their cries of pain ringing in his ears. The French forces easily outnumbered the English soldiers gathered here. His heart pounded loudly, and he knew it wise to retreat before more casualties occurred.

"Could it be any worse?" Robert shouted through his helmet, above the din.

They'd abandoned their horses in favor of their feet. Dace quickly appeared to spirit the animals from harm's way. Gavin had abandoned his shield and now yielded his sword in one hand, his mace in the other, both clutched tightly as he made good use of them.

"Fall back!" The order sounded several times across the battlefield. He sensed the English forces gradually moving behind him.

He signaled Robert. Both men retreated, only swinging their swords a time or two. It seemed like fighting would be called off for the day.

They arrived back where they'd started so many hours ago. Gavin pulled the heavy helmet from his head, every muscle in his arms and back strained to their limits, calling for respite.

Dace ran up, his face betraying bad news. All color had rushed from it, leaving the squire deathly pale. Out of breath, he stopped before them, his breath coming in long gasps.

"Easy, Dace," he told the squire. He reached for a wineskin and offered it to the young man. "Drink slowly. Your news 'twill keep."

Dace did as instructed, dribbling wine down the front of his tunic despite Gavin's warning. He did not venture to speak until he could be understood.

"'Tis a bargain the Black Prince stands to make." Dace pushed his hair from his brow with a forearm. "The French force has overwhelmed us, my lord. His advisers said that to maintain dignity, much less leave with our lives, 'twould be the only way. 'Tis too many we are up against."

"What says this bargain?" asked Robert.

Dace shook his head, his mouth gone sour. "The Prince himself wrote it. Called for parchment and ink, he did. Said 'twould come from his hand and his alone, to go straight to King John the Good." The squire spat in the dust. "He means to leave French soil. Not to fight for seven years."

"Seven years?" echoed Gavin. He'd known how heavily they were outnumbered in the field this day, but to leave France for so long a time? That might prove a disaster in the long run.

"And," Dace continued, "the prisoners already taken are to be surrendered, along with the spoils won."

He quickly cut his eyes to Robert. Both men realized with Dace's words how desperate the situation had become.

"I wonder how soon 'twill take King John to reply?" mused Robert.

Gavin raked his fingers through his hair, a nervous gesture he'd never been able to rid himself of. "I doubt we'll wait long. With their advantage, France would do well to press it quickly."

Rumors circulated the camp for less than two hours before word reached them. Again, Dace brought it, his mouth a thin line as he hurried toward them. It struck Gavin how young the boy seemed at that moment.

"France has rejected all," the squire revealed. "Ye

must be quick, my lord. Even now, French knights advance on foot."

Gavin had anticipated such news, not trusting the French to back down so easily. He and Robert had readied their rested destriers, and they now mounted them quickly. He checked to see that he had all the weapons he required, daggers and swords, his shield, and his mace.

"My lord?"

He looked down at his squire, who held his helmet high. "The mail coif will do, Dace. I'd like as much vision about me as I can."

"But, my lord—"

"No buts, Dace." He winked at the boy, trying to bolster his own courage as he reassured the squire. His heart hammered in his chest as loudly as the cannons that had gone off at Crecy. He touched his hand to his head and gave a brief nod before turning his horse.

He and Robert rode through a field of blood. Heavy losses had occurred. Gavin blocked out the agonizing calls for help, the pitiful cries, the torn and mangled bodies that lay all about them on the battlefield. The smell of blood filed the air, heavy now with despair, as they joined up with others who resumed the fight.

Then they were upon a large group of French foot soldiers, and his concentration began in earnest. He fought from atop his destrier for some minutes, the height giving him some small advantage. While distracted to his left, though, an enemy soldier plunged his sword high into the throat of the horse Gavin rode.

As he heard the gurgling scream, the horse started to falter. He threw a leg over and leapt from the beast before it took him down. A primeval shout poured from his mouth as he swung his mace. It connected with the head of the offending Frenchman. The man dropped dead to the ground, his own scream trailing off before he made contact with the dirt.

Gavin threw himself into the fight full force, his sword punishing every man in his path. His ears rang with the musical clanging of sword against sword, sword upon shield. Sweat dripped into his eyes, stinging them, clouding his vision for a moment.

It reassured him that Robert fought next to him. No braver man had Gavin met than his friend. If they came out of this, 'twould be together. If one fell, the other would catch him. And if by chance they died this day, they would know they had taken a good number of French bastards into death with them.

Robert brushed up against his back suddenly. Gavin looked over his shoulder to see they were slowly being surrounded. Back-to-back they fought, lashing out at those who pressed closely.

Robert roared an obscenity.

"What's wrong?" answered Gavin, forcing his sword into another man's chest, then ripping it from the body as his foot kicked the man lifeless body away.

"The bloody fool sliced my arm. God's wounds, but it hurts."

"The right or left?" called Gavin, knowing Robert was left-handed.

"'Tis my left," Robert muttered.

He stole a quick glance and saw the bright stream of blood pouring down Robert's arm, which now hung at his side. His friend's shield thrusted upward, warding off blows. Gavin knew with Robert's injury that their time was running out.

As he turned back, a dark swirl met him. Blind-sided, the shot caused the world to go stark white. As Gavin blinked several times, trying to get his bear-ings, a curtain of darkness began to descend.

His world went black.

3

Gavin groaned. His hands went to his pounding head. His fingers immediately touched dried blood matted through the back of his scalp. Gradually, he remembered the battlefield. The hoarse cries. The carnage. His magnificent destrier's throat gushing blood.

And Robert? *Where was Robert?*

He forced open his eyes. The barest of light filled the room he occupied. His head ached tremendously, as did the muscles across his shoulders and through his lower back. His gaze swept across the surroundings. He decided to sit up.

Immediately, a flash of light rippled across the room. It brought intense pain. He cradled his head in his hands and took long, deep breaths, willing the agony to recede.

It did. He knew it would. He wasn't injured enough. Robert was another matter, though. Gavin remembered the deep slice across his friend's upper arm and the long trail of dripping blood as the limb hung uselessly at his side. He took his time and lifted his head carefully before he gradually rose to his feet. The room was sparse. A table with a wooden bench on each side held a lone candle and basin. Gavin scanned the room and saw another cot. Robert lay upon it.

His friend was sleeping—or unconscious. He still wore his aketon. Gavin looked down at himself, noting his hauberk was gone. Only the thickly padded aketon remained. Obviously, the chain mail could have been used as a weapon. Their captors had stripped them of that.

What of Robert's wound? Gavin bent and touched his friend's left arm. He flinched, a frown crossing his flushed face. Gavin brought his open palm to Robert's forehead. Fever burned within him.

Nothing had been done about Robert's injury, and Gavin had not even a small baselard to cut away the cloth and see to the wound. At least the aketon's thickness had helped stanch the bleeding. Still, Robert's arm needed to be bathed and the injury stitched and dressed in clean cloth.

A metal scraping broke the silence. The door suddenly swung open and an old priest entered, a basket over his arm. He grunted something in French, and the door closed behind him. Gavin heard the lock turn.

He met the eyes of the bearded cleric. This man had done nothing to harm him. Gavin hoped the cleric was here to tend to Robert's arm—and not to give last rites.

He pushed the thought far away. He would not let his companion die.

The priest moved across the room until he stood in front of them, speaking in heavily-accented English. "I am Father Janus."

Gavin moved closer and inclined his head. "Sir Gavin Garwood of Ashgrove." He motioned to the cot.

"This is Sir Robert of Fondren. He's been injured in the battle." Gavin indicated the arm, its cloth crusted with dried blood.

"Yes. His injury is why I am here." The old priest, so tall and thin, knelt beside Robert as if to pray.

He bit his tongue. A pretty prayer might be all well and good, but Robert's damaged limb needed attention now.

Father Janus set down the basket and opened it. His movements were slow and deliberate as he cut the cloth from Robert's arm. Peeling the material away, the priest studied the injury some moments.

"The water, please." He spoke slowly, deliberately, as if thinking of every word, translating before he voiced it.

Gavin went to the table. The bowl contained water. He brought it back to the priest.

"May I help?" he asked as he rested the bowl on the ground next to the cot.

The cleric nodded. "Hold him. Stay out of my way. I do not wish to harm him more than he has already suffered."

Gavin dropped to his knees and kept Robert still as the priest cleansed the wound, first with water and then using wine from a small flask he produced. He then cracked an egg and rubbed the white from it onto the wound.

Bending close to the gash, he held the wound closed and chanted, "In the name of the Father, Son, and Holy Mary. The wound was red, the cut deep, the flesh be sore, but there will be no more blood or pain till the blessed Virgin bears a child again."

The priest then reached into the basket once more. He brought out a poultice. He placed it upon the wound and then bandaged it, winding a clean cloth around the arm multiple times to hold the poultice in place. Robert moaned a few times, but Gavin thought his friend wouldn't remember any of this.

Father Janus gave him a few instructions and left the basket behind. "They will bring soup soon. See that he takes some. Water, too, will help keep his fever down."

Gavin helped the priest to his feet. He was amazed at how little skin was wrapped around the man's bones. If he would have but squeezed, the bones would have snapped and turned to dust in his hands.

"*Merci.*" Father Janus studied him. "They mean to ransom you. The English caused heavy losses for France today. They need more money to fight these idiotic wars. They will not let you die."

His words reassured Gavin. Due to their armor and clothing, he and Robert would have stood out as nobility. Ransoming the enemy was common practice among many countries. As soon as he could get a missive off, the process would be in motion. It would take several weeks to get a message to England and their respective homes, his in the northern border country, Robert's to the south.

But in time, they would go home. Gavin's relief stirred him to care for Robert all the more. They would make it through this. Together.

He watched the priest leave the room. The old man gave him a brief smile before he left.

Gavin pulled one of the benches over to Robert's cot and seated himself next to his friend.

Robert would come through this. He must.

––––––––––––

"Are you cheating again?"

Robert cocked one eyebrow. "Me? Cheat?" He sighed. "Mayhap I'm simply changing the rules of the game somewhat."

Gavin smiled indulgently at his friend. It had been touch and go for a good fortnight, but Robert had recovered from his wound. Amazingly enough, no infection set in. Whatever poultices Father Janus pulled from his bag on a daily basis had done the trick. After close to two months, Robert was the picture of health, thanks to the simple country fare they'd eaten. Gavin had no idea how the priest connected to this puzzle, but he felt certain the man was responsible for their fair treatment.

He moved his chess piece and tried to hide a triumphant smile. "Check."

"God's wounds, Gavin. How can you expect me to win if I do not cheat? You constantly check here and there and then 'tis checkmate on top of that. Do you realize I have won but two bloody matches in all the time we have been here?"

Gavin laughed heartily. "You have not the patience to plan your moves, Robert. Chess is a game of strategy. You must think ahead four, eight, even twelve moves. Never be predictable. The way to win is to outthink your opponent. Lull him into complacency. Then," and he allowed a smile to grace his face, "go in for the kill."

Robert pushed back from the table and began pacing the small room they had been confined to. "All well and good for *you* to say. You have a military mind. Me? I have the brute strength to be nothing more than a good soldier. Go where I am told, when I am told, and kill the enemy. I may be a knight, but I am only a simple farmer at heart."

Gavin stood, as well. "I've seen Fondren, my friend. 'Tis no simple estate, and you are no simple farmer." He sighed. "'Twould that we would have been known to each other all those years ago whilst I fostered with Lord Aldred."

Robert grimaced. "Aye, I would have liked that, too. Instead I was freezing my love-apples off in the unforgiving north."

Gavin gave his friend a mock look of horror. "Take care, Robert of Fondren. You tread on sacred ground. Those of us born in the north have it in our blood, all our lives, no matter where our travels take us."

His friend laid a hand on Gavin's shoulder. "And being a border lad, I bet you fancy the fine comfort of our accommodations here. 'Twould be a step up from your usual way."

Gavin looked over the sparse room and chuckled. "Not that I won't be ready to be ransomed. The sooner, the better." He paused. "I wonder how much longer 'twill take."

Robert closed his eyes in thought. "You know it takes several weeks just to get the message to the coast and back through the channel and bay. Not as long for my father to receive, being closer in Kent."

He opened his eyes and grinned. "Why, 'twould not surprise me if the French messenger gives up when he sees how harsh and unforgiving the north is. He will fairly run screaming for London and a ship back to France."

Robert winked. "'Twill mean that I, of course, will be ransomed first. But not to worry, Gavin. I am sure they will eventually come hunting for you. Why, without my fine, calming influence, you may become a veritable madman. Our captors will probably chase you to the sea and cheer when you dive into the rough channel waters and swim for home."

Gavin slapped Robert on the back. He probably would have already gone mad if not for the company of his friend. Being enclosed in the single, tiny space for so long made him restless. He prayed again that the ransom would arrive soon. He didn't know how much more he could take of such confinement.

A light knock sounded at the door, followed by the turning key. Father Janus appeared in the doorway, as thin as ever. Gavin thought the man might blow away on a strong wind.

"Have you ever thought about stealing a bite now and then from the food you bring us?" he asked.

The priest looked up in surprise. "Steal? Why, I have taken a vow of poverty, my boy."

Gavin shook his head as Robert coughed politely into his hand. Something was lost in the translation. Mayhap he could remedy that.

"Would you care to join us, Father, and dine with us?"

The cleric thought it over a moment. "No, I have much yet to do. But I thank you for the invitation." He pulled a large loaf of bread from his sack and placed it on the table. Next came a round of cheese and a portion of fish.

"You are good to us, Father," Gavin told him as he broke off a bite of the bread.

"Only God is good, my son. We are simply placed upon this earth to try and imitate His goodness." He brightened. "Your boredom may be coming to an end."

Both he and Robert looked up expectantly.

The priest laughed heartily. "A letter arrived a

short while ago with a seal of blood red, embossed with a—"

"—lion," finished Robert. "So, my father received the ransom note and has replied."

"Yes. You are to be set free come the morn. I must go now, but I wanted to share such good news with you." He pulled a parchment from his bag. "A letter from your father, my boy. Enjoy reading it."

"Thank you." Robert took the old priest's hand and dropped to his knees before him. "Thank you for caring so well for us."

"My pleasure," Father Janus replied. He looked at Gavin with raised brows. "I did not take a vow to give up the pleasure in helping others."

As he left, Gavin realized he might have many more weeks before his freedom came. Robert must have thought of the same thing.

"I'll stay with you, Gavin, until your ransom arrives."

He saw the depths of sincerity in Robert's warm gaze. "I thank you, but I won't keep you from your simple farm. 'Tis sure that the pigs need slopping and the cows milking. I would not want to keep you from such enjoyable endeavors."

In the end the two men sat up all night, talking of their homes and their dreams for the future. Robert had improvements he wanted to make around Fondren, pending his father's approval. Gavin wanted to try a new strain of cattle at Ashgrove, one he believed would weather the elements better and whose meat would be even tastier.

"I pledge my eternal friendship to you, Gavin," Robert told him as dawn broke and a thin shaft of light made its way into the room. "There's nothing I would not do for you, my friend. Know that."

The two men embraced and remained silent until Robert left. When the time came, all words had been spoken between them, so Gavin raised a hand in farewell. Robert nodded and left the room without a backward glance.

The day dragged as slow as poured honey with only himself for company. Robert always had an interesting story, a tale from his youth or one he'd heard a minstrel perform. Gavin realized just how keenly he would miss his friend.

When he awoke on the seventeenth day after Robert left, it was to the rattling of the key in the lock. Gavin sat up expectantly. Finally, his time was at hand. He sensed it in his bones.

It was not Father Janus, though. Gavin had expected it to be the priest that brought him the good news. Instead, an overweight guard with fewer teeth than a babe thrust a missive in his hand.

Gavin fingered the broken seal lovingly, his first connection with Ashgrove in such a long time. Gingerly, he opened the letter and scanned its brief contents.

He read it again. Panic made his heart thunder. Then, thinking hearing it aloud would change its contents, he quietly mumbled, "The answer is no. No ransom from Ashgrove will be forthcoming. Do with your prisoner as you see fit."

It was signed by his father's hand.

4

Gavin awoke to another day in hell. The rodent-infested cell remained dank, dark, and dirty. Just like yesterday. Just like the day before that. Just like it would be tomorrow.

He fought the bitterness that blanketed him every waking moment. He thought about his mother. She would never recognize him. His once fine battle wear now hung in rags about him. His black hair was greasy, matted, and full of lice. A thick beard covered his face.

For the thousandth-plus-one time, he wondered why his father had refused to ransom him once he'd received the demand from his French captors. He couldn't fathom why it happened. Why he was left to rot in prison. He ran through the list he composed on a daily basis, which only served to torture him.

Had his father actually received his missive? Had he sent the gold, only to have it intercepted by brigands?

Yet Gavin saw with his own eyes the note delivered from Ashgrove. The seal broken, his father's handwriting within. Why such a betrayal? Why such malice?

As always, interminable questions—and no answers.

His thoughts turned back to his beloved mother. Was Gillian in good health? Or had she died? She had always been frail and often ill. Would that incident have driven his father mad with grief, even to the point where he didn't know what he did, and refused to bring his own son home? He doubted it. He'd never witnessed any affection, much less love, between his parents, only a veiled politeness.

And he also knew of his father's many mistresses. Berwyn Garwood was not one to be without a woman, especially since his wife spent far too much time in the drafty chapel on her knees in long hours of prayer, day after day, happy to be with her God.

Gavin had almost given up on there even being a God. Why would He leave him here to rot for two long years? Every day alive was Hell on earth, all hours awake spent miserably in the cold and damp. Gavin looked forward to the small bits of food, only to be disappointed every time it arrived. *When* it came, that is.

He let his mind take him away to a feast at Ashgrove. They proved even bigger and better than those he'd witnessed while fostering under Lord Aldred at Kentwood. Gavin noticed how his father had started many of the same traditions as the man he had fostered under, only turning them more magnificent and costly. If he ever escaped, Gavin would never take any feast—or any morsel of food—for granted again.

Often, he wondered what Lord Aldred would do in this situation. Survival would be paramount, of course. The warrior had instilled in Gavin from his youth that he could do anything. The great warrior trained him not only physically, but toughened Gavin mentally.

He had tried to escape. It was his duty to king and country. He had more than a half-dozen failed attempts behind him. One resulted in injuring three guards. He'd almost made it to daylight that time.

How sweet 'twould be to see a sunrise! To have the warmth of the summer sun upon his face once again. All the little things, the small freedoms and odd moments taken for granted, he'd now come to savor while in captivity.

He bore the scars of his efforts. He supposed by now his back was a collage from the multiple whippings and beatings. They'd slammed his hand in something once. He couldn't remember now, but the little finger on his left hand had never healed properly. It now jutted out at an odd angle. As punishment, they shackled him to the wall for months. At least he could move about some now, for which he gave thanks.

The most severe beating had left permanent damage. So many heavy blows about his head, the blood pouring freely from his ear. A ringing that lasted for days upon end... then... silence. He no longer could hear from his left ear.

He tried to stay strong, despite the meager diet provided. He worked his muscles each day, which proved difficult at times. The cell, though fairly large, held several men within it at any given point. He learned to have no qualms about taking food from those so ill they would never eat again. Better him than the rats. Anything to stay strong and be ready for the day he would break the shackles of this place and find sweet freedom.

He waited and watched for opportunity. Gavin

knew the guards' names. Their routines. The ones that seemed fair. The ones who abused their limited authority. He would be ready when the next opportunity for escape came.

It would be the last time, for if he failed in his attempt, he would go mad. Dying would be preferable.

He heard someone coming. He lifted his good ear toward the noise. He recognized Gustave's voice, which meant he brought Father Janus with him. Gustave was the only one who would call for the priest whenever last rites needed to be delivered. He looked over at the man whose breath rattled noisily in his chest. He no longer bothered to learn the names of new prisoners. They didn't matter.

The guard and priest turned the corner. Gavin was grateful for the nominal friendship he had with the cleric. On more than one occasion, Father Janus had palmed a bread crust to him, sometimes even a piece of hard cheese. Once, upon Christmas, the priest had even smuggled Gavin a fistful of precious meat.

As Father Janus entered the cell today, he gave Gavin the familiar, comforting smile. Gavin found a smile now held the same value to him as a well-trained destrier or a large bag of gold. Little things held the true measure of worth. He might have been vain before, enjoying fine clothes and living in a grand keep on a massive estate, but he'd discovered there was so much more to life. A man's good name, the small kindnesses he bestowed upon others, a rainbow after a summer shower—all these proved priceless to him.

Father Janus pulled back his cowl. Immediately, it struck Gavin how sunken the priest's eyes were. Where the priest had always been tall and forever thin, he now appeared gaunt beyond measure. When had Gavin last seen him? Had it been a month? Two?

The holy man signaled for him to come close, even as Gustave motioned the prisoner needing to receive the last rites was in the far back corner. Gavin followed as Gustave left. The stench here proved even worse. Foul smells and piles of vomit surrounded what was left of the man's living body. Even after so long a time here, it was hard for Gavin to face the squalid conditions.

Others in the cell wasted away, too. Many slept. No one paid attention as Gavin touched the priest's shoulder, wondering what he wanted.

"I'm dying," the old man told him, his voice just above a whisper. "I feel it in my bones. I can't eat anymore. Days have gone by without my holding down even the simplest crust of bread."

Gavin ached as the priest shared this news with him. He feared once Father Janus passed, then no one from the outside world would ever come again to this prison. This kind man of God had been Gavin's link to goodness for so long. The priest had become Gavin's only friend and a lifeline that held the fragile bit of Gavin's sanity in place. He dreaded what might happen when the priest was gone.

"Even water will not stay down," the cleric continued. "Aches in my joints, to my very bones. I awoke and somehow knew this was my last day on earth."

Gavin watched as the priest slid down the wall he leaned against and sighed. "God will welcome me into His loving arms, but He wishes me to do one last act of mercy." He reached up and took Gavin's hand. "I am to help you, my son, before I leave this earth."

Father Janus began intoning the Latin words of the last rites over the dying prisoner, words which even now soothed Gavin in some odd way. Lord Aldred forced him to learn Latin and Greek as a boy. They had worked on some German, but Gavin found it harder to understand and remember such a guttural language.

Suddenly, the words ceased. The priest whispered, "Do you know Latin? Can you imitate me?"

He nodded, a little unsure since it had been so long. The priest started off, and he followed his lead, taking over. Gavin didn't know the entire ritual, but he thought he could fake it. Who would know? The guards were uneducated, and none were even in sight.

Father Janus stood and took off his cloak, then began to shed his garments. He indicated for Gavin to do the same. As Gavin murmured the Latin words, they switched clothing and re-dressed themselves. Gavin was in shock. He didn't think they could pull off such a deception.

He switched to passages from Homer. He figured it was close enough, and he was much more familiar with it since it had been a boyhood favorite of his. As he spoke, the priest whispered to him and instructed him on exactly what to do.

5

Gustave appeared. Gavin's knees quaked. The guard unlocked the cell door, though, not even passing a cursory glance in his direction, and simply motioned him out.

Gavin tried to move slowly, as if he were the elderly priest. He in no way wanted to tip his hand to the Frenchman. As he began to shuffle along in Father Janus's familiar gait, he realized he didn't know the way out from this prison.

He'd been brought here unconscious from the place he and Robert had originally been kept when they were hostages to be ransomed. Gavin had fought the guards that came to remove him from that long-ago place of simple comfort, not knowing if he went to his death.

How would he find the direction he should take?

As he moved along the dark hallway, lit only by a few torches, he saw a staircase in front of him. He'd never made it this far before in his escape attempts. Excitement rushed through him. He could hear the pounding of blood in his right ear. He quelled the tremble in his limbs and followed Gustave up the stairs.

At the top, the guard unlocked the door and pushed it open. Gavin kept his head bowed, the cowl pulled over his head and held close to his face. He stepped through the door without pausing. Behind him the clang of metal and the grinding of a lock echoed. It was the sound of locking steel that almost unnerved him. His knees buckled, and he stumbled. He threw out a hand and clutched at the wall. No one saw him, though. The long passageway before him was empty.

He followed it to daylight. *The sun!* How long had it been since he'd seen it? He kept his joy in check, though, and continued in a slow shuffle. The dark cowl pulled over his head remained close, his face all but invisible, as he counted each step.

Then he was free. Gavin stepped through an unlocked door. Outside, a crisp wind blew in the open courtyard. Clasping the worn robe tightly about him, he looked simply as if he prepared to face the elements. He harnessed the feelings of exultation, his movements slow and deliberate, not wanting to call attention to himself in any way. At the gate, a guard called out to him.

"Greetings, Father!"

Panic filled him. He understood and even spoke French, but he sounded nothing like Father Janus. The minute he acknowledged the gatekeeper, the ruse would be discovered.

He stopped at the gate and waved up at the guard. His alarm spread as the man motioned to his companion and began descending the ladder, coming straight for him. Fear rippled through his body at the thought of being caught and returned to his hellhole. He would go down fighting and welcome death before returning to that cell.

In desperation, he offered up a last, desperate prayer to God to see him through this ordeal. He held the cowl more closely and dipped his head.

The man arrived before him and rattled off several sentences in a thick, peasant dialect. Gavin only caught a few phrases, but he surmised the guard had a sick daughter. He wanted the priest to accompany him to his hut.

He saw no way out of the situation, so he nodded. If need be, he would kill this guard in the privacy of his home before he would allow the man to sound an alarm. The sentinel turned and hurried off. Gavin followed at a much slower pace, staying in character.

The hut wasn't but a hundred paces from the prison's gate. He suppressed the desire to wrap his arm about the guard's neck and snap it. He hoped he could go through the motions this man expected to see and hear and successfully continue his escape attempt.

As they entered the man's home, Gavin was hit by smells from long ago—a warm fire crackling noisily, stew bubbling in a cauldron, rushes on the floor. Underneath, however, permeated the smell of death, something he was all too familiar with these past two years during his imprisonment.

He saw a young girl about four years of age, lying upon a pallet near the fire. Tiny and blond, her unnatural brightness told him she was flushed with fever. He went to her and knelt. Taking her hand, he smiled at her.

In that moment a powerful connection was forged. Gavin sensed it running through their linked fingers. "What is your name, child?" he asked her in French, deliberately keeping his voice in a whisper.

She smiled weakly at him, her eyes full of hope. "Lisette."

He began to speak in Latin then, soft and low, as he rested his palm against her brow. For some minutes he told her of Odysseus and how revered he was far and wide. He told her of the great journey Odysseus would embark upon and how it would cost him what was most dear. Lisette began to drift off to sleep.

When he would go, she held tightly onto his hand for a moment, her eyes closed but a smile upon her thin lips. The gesture moved Gavin. He felt more alive than he had since that last day on the battlefield. To have contact, to be treated as a human being and not an animal, brought tears to his eyes.

He squeezed her hand in return, and gradually Lisette dropped off to sleep. She looked so peaceful resting before the fire. He made the sign of the cross over her and stood.

The guard, who'd remained by the door, thanked him over and over. Gavin mumbled in Latin, "The pig jumped over the fence, chased by the fox." It was the only phrase that came to mind. He made the sign of the cross again and left, not daring to look back.

"Don't hurry," he muttered under his breath. "Pace yourself."

The wind chilled him as he walked. Did he used to notice things such as that before, or was it all war, wenches, and wine? At least the cold ache of his numb fingers let him know he was alive.

He reached the outskirts of a town and had to cross through it to reach where Father Janus had told him the horse lay in wait. He listened to snippets of conversation as he shuffled along but never caught the name of where he was. He longed to stop and speak with someone, touch someone, as he had little Lisette.

Yet he realized no stopping could be allowed. He couldn't wonder what was happening in the war or if his squire Dace now fought for England on the battlefield. He wouldn't think about his family, which brought an ache and keen sense of betrayal. He must get out. He must find the horse and make his escape from France.

He must survive.

He no longer knew how much time had passed. Had he walked an hour or the entire afternoon? What if the old priest had been out of his head as his life ebbed away? Gavin shuddered and pushed everything aside except the need to go on.

He reached a wooded area and heard the sound of running water with his good ear. He dared not look about him as he ventured into the woods at the maddeningly slow pace that he forced himself to keep. The sound of the water grew louder, and then the brook appeared. Gavin walked to the water's edge and plunged his hands into the clear stream.

The frigid water numbed his hands instantly, but that didn't stop him. He greedily drank his fill of the water and then splashed it over his face and neck, knowing it would take heated water and hours of scrubbing to remove the layers of grime. Reluctant to leave the stream, he let the chilled water run across his hands until they lost all feeling, trying to remove some of the filth buried deeply in his flesh. He must be a fright. Perhaps he could pass himself off as a priest gone mad. He could roar in Latin to keep others away.

Gavin drank again. Never would anything again taste as good to him as the water from this brook. He stood at last and crossed to the opposite bank, ready to search for the promised horse.

Then he heard the cry for help. He froze, unsure what to do. But the sound was fairly insistent. As if his feet had a mind of their own, he turned in the direction of the noise. In a set of thorned bushes, he spied the mewling kitten, struggling to be freed. Without thought to the pain, Gavin reached into the bramble and pulled the scrawny animal to safety.

He brought it close to inspect it, and the kitten leaned its paws upon his shoulders and nuzzled his neck, purring loudly in thanks. The gesture of gratitude did him in. He collapsed in a heap, bringing his knees close to his chest. He cradled the kitten and cried, blubbering like a babe or jilted lover. Great tears fell down his cheeks and onto the small fur ball, who began kneading its paws into him.

He set the grateful creature down and wiped his eyes, but still more tears came. The kitten jumped back into his lap and scrambled to his chest. It leaned up, its paws going once again onto his shoulders. This time a sandpaper tongue darted out and began to lick the tears from his cheeks. Gavin stroked the thin animal, who gave him unfettered love.

He picked up the tiny creature and stroked its fur. Though Gavin could feel the animal's ribs and its coat was as dirty as his rags, the kitten looked like a fighter. It was a smoky gray with large, amber eyes. He supposed it wandered off from its mother or had even been abandoned. In that instant, he hitched his fate to the kitten. If it survived, so would he. He would do whatever it took to keep this small furball alive. He was a little superstitious in that respect.

With the purring cat cradled in his palm, Gavin set out to find the horse. When he did, it looked as scrawny and underfed as his new pet. He hoped the animal would carry his weight. He had to find out now where he was and where he could go. Mounting the horse, he lightly kicked its sides and took off. He breathed in the fresh air.

It was the first day of his new life.

6

KENTWOOD—1358

"Lord Aldred has a wish for blancmanger, Cook. But less almonds and more sugar this time, I think," Elizabeth mused, considering how her husband was beginning to have difficulty in chewing. She'd also be sure the chicken in the dish was thinly sliced before Aldred received it.

"And some frumenty pudding," she added.

The toothless woman grinned. "Ye needn't worry, me lady. I'll take fine care of his lordship. Best be about me business then."

Cook ambled off, her large girth shifting from side to side as she hobbled back to the kitchens.

Elizabeth signaled to Nelia, and the servant glided over.

"How is Lord Aldred today, my lady? He is in my prayers every night."

"Better than yesterday. These bouts with his belly are tiresome for him, though. He got very little sleep last eve."

"And for you, my lady?" Nelia observed Elizabeth carefully, her eyebrows raised. "Shouldn't you get some rest yourself?"

She sighed. Nelia had tried to mother her ever since she arrived at Kentwood half a score ago.

"I'm well, Nelia. You needn't coddle me. I'm a grown woman of eight-and-twenty, not a small child. Let's see to today's business."

She patted the servant's shoulder, not wanting the woman to be upset. "First, I'd like the sweeping and mopping to occur throughout the downstairs, and then fresh rushes laid in the great hall. We also need to churn more butter, and I want to check on our candle supply. We may have to make more a little ahead of what we had previously planned."

After running through her list of tasks to accomplish that day, Elizabeth added, "I will be with Cedd if you need me. That will be all."

She ignored the look Nelia shot her way. The servant had worked inside the castle walls all her life and thought her mistress handling the accounts was most unladylike. Domestic chores and needlework were all Nelia deemed acceptable for a noblewoman to do.

Yet how would Kentwood have survived if she hadn't stepped in?

Cedd waited for her in the room where all estate business originated. He smiled at his mistress, his good eye directly upon her. The other wandered off in all directions. It had unsettled her when she'd first arrived at her husband's home, but she soon learned what a decent man and hard worker Cedd was and how much Aldred depended upon Cedd's experience and advice. Now she rarely noticed the problem.

"Good morning, my lady. We have much to discuss."

Elizabeth shot him a concerned look. "Is there a problem I'm not aware of?"

"Nay, my lady," Cedd reassured her. "Three good harvests in a row? All is going smoothly. But there are a few matters that will need your prompt attention."

Hours later, she tipped her head back and then from side to side, stretching the muscles in her neck that ached from the time bent over the accounts.

"I'm satisfied for now, Cedd, and 'tis my time to spend with Lord Aldred." She stood. "Would you have Nelia check the wood supply?"

"I will check it myself, my lady." The steward pushed back his chair and stood. "You take on too much. I will see that 'tis done and to your usual standards."

Elizabeth nodded. "Thank you, Cedd." She left the room, running her fingers through her hair, trying to smooth down the unruly curls. She broke with tradition and rarely wore a veil inside the castle. Aldred thought her auburn hair too beautiful to be hidden.

She smiled at the thought of pleasing her husband with such a simple gesture. After so long a time together, she looked fondly upon him and hoped she'd brought a spark of happiness to his final years. He'd taught her so much. How to read and write. To read even Latin, and better than any priest. They conversed in French regularly, and Aldred claimed she sounded like a native. If the French should ever invade southern England because of this bloody war, she'd spy upon them and see that every Frenchman that landed anywhere in the whole of Kent would be drawn and quartered.

Moreover, Aldred indulged her in many ways. She hunted now, and had a keener sense than most men as to when and where a prey would move. She oversaw the accounts. She visited their tenants and knew every name, down to each small babe, the last born only two days before.

Elizabeth overcame her fears and now assisted in childbirths across the estate. She still was uncomfortable with the idea, but she realized it would never be her turn to give birth. This helped her detach from the process, and she'd become quite skilled at midwifery. After all, it was expected of Lord Aldred's wife. The people looked to her for leadership and assurance. She'd learned to be strong in all areas.

Her husband had even turned over disputes to her. When the people gathered once a month, she and Aldred sat together to hear their petitions, but it was now Elizabeth who made every decision on her own. In the beginning, Aldred started by guiding the judgments in private.

He had his wife tell him her reasoning when she arrived at a solution. Eventually satisfied with her sound conclusions, he pronounced all rulings would come from her. Elizabeth learned to stand upon keen listening and to trust her own common sense when announcing her decisions regarding disputes.

She had made a good wife to her husband. The only place she had failed him was in keeping his children alive. His eldest son had died in battle before their marriage, and the second boy fell from his horse during a hunt. Only five-and-ten, he'd lost the use of both his legs and arms. 'Twas a painful two years he spent before dying of a fever, and she'd agonized that she couldn't save the genial young man.

Aldred's only daughter succumbed to the same fever at ten-and-four. Elizabeth did everything she could, staying day and night with the girl as she slowly wasted away. After that, the spirit seemed to go out of her husband, especially knowing they would not have any children of their own. She was grateful, though, not to endure lying with him. The few kisses they'd shared behind closed doors, meant to be intimate, only repulsed her. She would grimace inwardly but put a brave smile on the outside.

She didn't mind his public displays of affection. He held her hand. Kissed her cheek. She liked the little kindnesses and truly had an affection for him. Knowing how wretched her life would have been if her father had made good and put her away in a convent made her appreciate Aldred's generosity all the more.

To think nuns took a vow of poverty. Elizabeth shuddered. She'd grown to enjoy the finer things in life. She had fertile land with good harvests, jewels, money, position, power. Why mumble prayers all day, performing menial tasks, when she could use her intelligence to succeed in a man's world? She had everything she wanted, her every wish fulfilled, the respect of her people.

Even the king had graced their table on several occasions and complimented her on how well things ran on the estate. No greater compliment could be received than from one's king.

She couldn't help but wonder just how Edward would treat her when Aldred died. That was the only sadness in her life, her husband's deteriorating health. She couldn't imagine life without him. He'd become friend, companion, and father to her.

With no heirs, though, what would come of her? Worse than a convent, Elizabeth would be miserable if the king decided to marry her to one of his favored knights. To have a stranger tell her what to do, after so many years of being in control of her own destiny? Impossible.

Yet that very real possibility loomed on the horizon.

"My lady?"

She turned as Nelia approached. "Yes?"

"A rider approaches from Fondren."

She smoothed her hunter green cotehardie. "'Twill be Sir Robert, more likely than not. He knows 'tis near the time that I visit my husband each day." She thought for a moment. "Fetch some stewed plums from the kitchens. I would take a treat to my good lord."

She turned and made her way outside to the inner bailey, spying Robert as he came through the courtyard.

He saw her and gave a wave before he dismounted and handed his reins to a groom. Bounding up the steps, he took her hands in his and pressed a quick kiss to her cheek.

"Radiant as always, Elizabeth. 'Tis no wonder neighboring knights write poetry to you and the wandering minstrels sing songs praising your beauty and intelligence." He gave her hands a squeeze and released them.

"And aren't you a neighboring knight? Why have you not joined my legion of admirers and written a love poem to me, my lord?"

Robert laughed. "'Tis atrocious at spelling I am, Elizabeth. I never lost myself in books the way you do. Now give me a sword if you were in distress, and I would slay any dragon that you beseeched me to."

She smiled. "You are a rascal, Robert." She cocked her head and studied him a moment. "'Tis a handsome one, though. I wish you would marry and give me a friend."

He shook his head. "Am I not a loyal friend to you as is? Nay, Elizabeth, I'm not so inclined."

He grew quiet, and she knew he must be thinking of his lost betrothed. She had died a week before their wedding took place, and Robert still deeply mourned the girl's passing.

"Then might you take a mistress, mayhap? I've never had a woman as companion before. Only men."

She suspected that was why she wanted to succeed in a man's world, for it was all she knew. She'd had no loving touch from a mother, so long dead that she had no remembrance of her.

Robert sputtered, "You are outrageous, Elizabeth."

She smiled. "And you wouldn't have me any other way, I suspect." She linked an arm through his. "Shall we go to Aldred now?"

"Yes. 'Tis why I've come." He frowned. "He sent a message earlier today for me to come see him."

His words puzzled her. "A message? I know of no message, Robert. Are you sure it came from Kentwood?"

"Yes, I recognized the boy who delivered it, and 'twas Aldred's seal upon it, unbroken." He gazed at her a long moment. "'Tis probably nothing. Let us go. Mayhap I spoke out of turn."

They climbed the stairs to the solar. Nothing happened at Kentwood that she did not know of. Why would Aldred wish to see Robert? He had looked favorably upon Robert over the years, and Robert had told her how much he respected Aldred's opinion. She wondered what was in the wind.

Knocking softly upon the door, she motioned Robert inside. They crossed the room. Aldred lay in the bed, his eyes closed. His peaceful look helped calm her concerns.

"My lord," she said quietly and went to stand by the bed.

Her husband opened his eyes and smiled when he recognized her. Elizabeth brushed the snow-white hair off his brow.

"I've brought Robert to see you," she told him. "We are here to visit you."

Robert stepped forward. "I trust you rested well today, my lord?"

Aldred snorted. "As much as a man can when his bones creak with every bend, his eyesight is poorer, and he has trouble swallowing anything needing more than four bites of chewing. I have not enough teeth left anymore to do the trick."

He looked at her with mock reproach. "My wife thinks to have my meat cut into little pieces, as if I don't know what she's up to."

She blushed. "But knowing you have caught onto my schemes, my lord husband, you'll find only small slivers of chicken in your blancmanger tonight. I've grown much more clever, I think."

Aldred laughed. He took her hand and rubbed his callused thumb in a small circle over it. "Tell Cook to chop it into the tiniest of bites. 'Twill end the charade and allow me to swallow in comfort."

He held his hands up before him. "These used to grip and swing the heaviest swords in the land. Now they can't even hold a candle still." He looked from her to Robert. "Don't grow old," he warned. "'Tis a terrible waste. Nothing works as well as it once did."

"At least you still possess your sense of humor, my lord," Robert pointed out. "A man withers and dies without one."

"Then I'll laugh to the grave. Probably even when I'm in it. And at least I'm blessed to still have my good sense, too. There are plenty..." Aldred's voice trailed off. Silence hung heavily in the room.

"Ah, my boy, forgive me," Aldred apologized. "I forget how your father fares."

"He has his good days and bad, I suppose," their guest said lightly.

A knock at the door was followed by Nelia entering. Elizabeth broke the tension in the room. "Ah, here are some stewed plums for you, my lord. I thought 'twould be just the thing for you to enjoy."

Her husband grimaced.

"Unless you'd prefer stewed pears or apples?" Nelia asked.

Elizabeth waved her away. "No, Nelia, that is all." The servant backed from the room as she took Aldred's hand. "'Twas a pain again, wasn't it?"

He nodded. "A bad one," he admitted. She knew how very bad it must have been to admit so in front of their visitor.

"Then I must be off," Robert said. "You are in good hands with Elizabeth to nurse you. May I call again on the morrow?"

"*No!*"

She was astonished at not only the volume but intensity in her husband's voice. She shot a quick glance at Robert.

"Stay," Aldred said, his breathing become more rapid.

"Of course." Robert returned to the bedside. "How might I assist you, my lord?"

Aldred glanced up at Elizabeth. "'Tis a private matter, my dear. I must speak with Robert alone."

Elizabeth was speechless. Aldred had never kept a

single secret from her. What could he possibly want from Robert that she couldn't know about?

"There's nothing that I can't do—or won't do—for you, Husband," she stated.

He smiled soothingly at her. "I know that, Wife. I will call if I have need of you. Now go and rest. You work far too hard."

She walked stiffly to the door, upset at the dismissal. She opened it and slipped out into the corridor.

What mysterious secret would Aldred share with Robert? And why?

7

ENGLAND—1359

Gavin kept his eyes on the sun as the first of it dipped below the horizon. Sunset had once been a favorite time of day for him. It meant an end to training exercises or battles in progress. Time for food and frolic. He could not remember how many countless women he'd pleasured himself with over the years. All those nights from long ago blurred as if they were one.

Nowadays, he treasured the sunrise instead. It was a sign that he was still alive and ready to take on a new day. The three months since his escape from the French hellhole had been harsh ones, first as he made his way to the coast, and then selling the horse for passage on a ship barely a step above his prison cell. Yet not a day dawned that he did not relish the life Father Janus had given back to him. He assumed the old priest died in the squalid cell even as Gavin escaped, allowing him to be reborn.

Northern England's landscape unfolded before him. Spring would bloom soon, but for now the last vestiges of winter hung over the land. Gavin inhaled deeply, enjoying the fresh smell of the clean, cold air and the look of trees that were on the verge of regaining their leaves.

He squatted and touched the soil beneath him, brushing his fingers along it reverently. English soil, which he would never take for granted again.

Homer voiced his displeasure, and he righted himself. He reached under the tattered cloak and stroked the growing kitten, resting in a sack he'd fashioned to hang from his neck. Homer nipped at his fingers playfully before snuggling close to him. The faint rumble of a purr began. Gavin wondered if it would take so little to appease him.

As twilight unfolded, feelings of apprehension filled him. Within a few miles, he would arrive at Ashgrove. He longed to see his parents, yet his stomach knotted with thoughts of that first meeting. Would he simply fall into his mother's arms as she wept with joy? Or would he push her aside and angrily confront his father? He'd had weeks to find an answer as he journeyed to Ashgrove and had yet to do so.

Once again, he thought that mayhap thieves apprehended the messenger en route and took the gold from him. Had the original courier been killed? Or had the man fled with the ransom? None of these explained the sealed note, though. Soon he would look into his father's eyes.

And find his answer.

Gavin arrived at the small village on Ashgrove lands. Already past dark, little activity occurred. Only a few scattered men were here and there, bringing in animals for the night.

One man passed close enough and looked at him oddly, probably due to Gavin's unkempt appearance. The thick, wild beard and knotted hair, along with clothes that were nearly rags, would frighten off anyone. Gavin hoped he would be recognized despite his disheveled appearance once he arrived home. He imagined trying to convince a new gatekeeper that he was the son of Ashgrove's lord. The thought caused him to chuckle, the first time he had done so in years.

As he approached the castle, excitement replaced trepidation. His heart beat rapidly. Butterflies swarmed his belly. He could barely swallow, so dry was his mouth. Homer seemed to sense his emotions and began to purr loudly, seeking to give him comfort.

At the gates, Gavin signaled to the men on duty and shouted at them, "'Tis I, Sir Gavin Garwood, come home from the wars in France. Open up."

Nothing happened. Surely, the watchmen had heard him?

He tried again, raising his voice in case it had been lost in the wind. "I say, open these gates. 'Tis Sir Gavin. I know you surely recognize my voice if not my face."

He watched as the two guards conferred. One disappeared. Gavin saw him seconds later when the gates opened slightly. He rushed over as the man stepped outside to greet him. The guard's eyes were wary, but he spoke to him all the same.

"'Tis good to see you alive, my lord."

He laughed and slapped the man on the back. "'Tis even better to be home. I know 'tis late, but please send a runner to awaken my mother. I would see her first and then speak with my father."

He started to walk toward the gate, but the guard stepped back, blocking his entrance. "You... you don't know?" The man began muttering and then turned quick as lightning, slipping through the gate.

Gavin reacted immediately and raced the few

steps as the opening began to vanish. "What's gotten into you, man? You can't keep me from my own home."

He pushed with all his remaining strength and forced the gate open. The guard pulled his sword and made an effort to stop him, but Gavin quickly grabbed the man's wrist and wrenched the weapon from the soldier's hands.

"Out of my way!" he roared. He would go to his father instead. This mess must be sorted out at once.

He crossed through the outer and inner baileys. No one followed him. All was quiet. He ran up the stairs of the keep, his heart hammering, unanswered questions filling his head. Silence blanketed the structure. He passed the great hall and saw a few servants bedded down by the fire, their bodies still in sleep. He finally passed one servant on the stairs. His face held what could only be described as a look of shock the moment he recognized Gavin. The man turned and raced back up the stairs and down the hallway. He assumed the servant went to awaken Berwyn.

He steeled himself for whatever showdown lay ahead. For a reason he didn't understand, he placed the sword against the wall when he reached the solar's door. He decided against knocking and threw open the door.

Firelight bathed the room in a golden glow. His father stood in a robe, his back to the fire, his own sword in hand. The curtains were pulled from the bed. Gavin saw a young woman peering out. Berwyn's women seemed to get younger each time. Gavin felt sorry for this girl and for his mother. He understood, though. Men had their needs. Gillian was very spiritual. He doubted his parents' relationship had remained physical for very long, especially since Gavin lacked in siblings.

He held out his hands, palms up. "I come unarmed, Father."

Taking a step forward, he watched Berwyn raise his sword, its tip pointed at Gavin's heart.

"What the Devil gives?" he demanded, his temper rising. "I almost died at the hands of those French bastards. Why did you not help me? Why do you stand there as if I am your sworn enemy? What's wrong, Father? I beg you to tell me."

"Leave at once," Berwyn said, his eyes full of hate. "You are no longer welcome at Ashgrove."

Gavin's throat grew tight. *What could he have done to earn such treatment?* "Why, Father? Why?"

Berwyn spat upon the ground. "Do not address me as such. You are not my son. Ashgrove will never belong to you."

Gavin's head spun. He heard the woman laugh harshly. He looked from her to his father. Confusion reigned.

"I don't understand."

"Tell him, my lord," purred the latest mistress. When no reply came, Gavin heard her voice grow hard. *"Tell him."*

Berwyn went and stood by the bed. The woman snaked out a hand and linked it possessively through his arm. Gavin saw a jeweled ring on her hand, one he could not be mistaken about.

"No." His denial came out a hoarse whisper.

"The babe that grows inside Clarine will be the son that inherits Ashgrove," Berwyn told him. *"My wife* is young and will give me plenty of sons in the years to come."

Words froze on Gavin's tongue. He sputtered, "But... but Mother—"

"That whore is dead," Berwyn bellowed. "Dead. And forgotten. As dead as you are to me. Now leave. You are trespassing."

Anger surged through him. "I will *not* leave. I demand you explain yourself, Father. My mother was not a whore. Not like the countless women who have shared your bed these many years."

Berwyn's lips snarled as he hissed, *"You are a bastard!* Can you not understand? You are not of my blood. I loathe the very sight of you, for you remind me of that deceitful bitch and her deception. Get out. Get out!"

Not of Berwyn's blood?

That meant his mother had lain with another man, before or soon after her marriage. Was this why she lost herself in prayer, day after day, trying to atone for such a powerful sin?

Gavin stumbled from the room, tripping over the sword left in the hallway. He ignored Homer's attempts at growling. He stooped and slipped the sword into his hand. This was real, a sword in his hand, a fight to be won. Not the lies that spilled from his father's mouth. He hurried down the stairs, passing several servants who had been awakened by their argument. He saw pity in their eyes as they stared at him before they turned away wordlessly.

As he reached the bottom of the staircase, he saw Eben, who'd put him on his first horse and taught him to ride. The stout servant locked strong fingers around Gavin's arm.

"Come with me," he whispered.

He pulled Gavin through the keep's halls until they reached outside. Gavin sucked in the sweet night air, hoping it would clear his head. Eben urged him on, and within minutes he found himself inside the stables of Ashgrove.

He collapsed upon a pile of straw, his breathing harsh. Eben lit a lantern and pulled up a stool next to him. Under his cloak, Homer wiggled in protest. Gavin reached in and pulled the kitten from his sack. Homer scurried off into the darkness.

"Don't talk, boy," Eben grumbled in low tones. "Just listen."

He stared at the servant, the homely face he'd known since his earliest memories, the man who'd taught him all he knew of animals. He nodded, wanting to hear why the world had gone mad.

"Your dear mother died nigh over two years ago, my lord. 'Twas not but a few weeks after you left for France." Eben shook his head sadly. "She was a true lady. All at Ashgrove do sorely miss her. With her passing, things changed."

The servant studied him. Gavin saw the hesitation on his face and urged, "Give me the truth, Eben. All of it."

Eben swallowed hard but continued. "Lord Ashton gathered the servants when her body was discovered. She'd been poorly for some days. It surprised no one when he announced her death.

"But," he added, "his next words startled everyone."

He paused, and Gavin spoke. "Go on."

"Lord Ashton announced he would marry on the morrow, after Lady Ashton's burial. He had her body placed far from where family should be buried, my lord. As if she were an outcast. Then he told us that you were not of his flesh and blood. That Lady Ashton deceived him for all these years and confessed on her

deathbed. He would not stand for it, nor would he let
you grace his presence ever again."

In the stillness of the night, Eben's words lingered. Gavin's mind fought the numbing shock set-
tling over it. He doubted his mother could behave in
such a manner. More than likely, his father wanted to
please the new mistress of Ashgrove and allow her
son to inherit the estate.

"We had standing orders if you ever turned up
again at Ashgrove, you were to be struck down upon
first sight." Eben mopped his brow. "No one could do
that, my lord. You are most beloved by your people
and innocent in this matter."

As he mulled over things in his mind, Gavin knew
it to be true. It would take more than simple misfor-
tune to turn a father away from his son. In that moment Gavin realized while he was away, Berwyn
Garwood had learned a truth that destroyed the ten-
uous relationship fostered with his son over a
lifetime.

And that meant Gavin's life as he knew it was
now over. He possessed no home. No family. No
money or land of his own. Where should he turn?

Instinctively, the answer came. He would go
south. To Lord Aldred. Aldred would know what to
do. Aldred would slice through the confusion and
help him see to the heart of the matter. Aldred would
give Gavin the advice he needed and shelter him.
Moreover, Robert's family lived nearby. Not only
would he have counsel from a man he greatly admired, but he knew he could count on his closest
friend for guidance, as well.

Gavin pulled himself to his feet. Exhausted after
so long a journey, another one, even longer, now
awaited him.

Eben must have seen the weariness in his eyes, for the servant spoke to him gently. "Come, my lord. I shall saddle you a horse. Even now, my wife and others gather clean clothes and food for you. I beg you. Never return here. Lord Ashton won't take kindly to those who disobeyed his orders and allowed you into Ashgrove tonight."

Gavin winced at the punishment the watchmen and others might face, all at his expense. He, more than most, knew the extent of Berwyn's wrath when stirred up.

"I cannot allow it, Eben. A missing horse? Father —Lord Ashton—will have your head for giving me the mount."

The servant touched a hand to Gavin's shoulder. "Nay, my lord. He shall never know. This is wrong, to be treated worse than an animal, thrown out with nothing. We mean to right things as best we can, for we know how he left you to suffer in that prison."

Before Gavin could protest, three men entered the stables.

"I'll saddle the horse, Eben. Here are clothes for Lord Gavin," said one. He quickly hurried away to ready the horse.

The other two smiled encouragingly at Gavin, both playmates of his nigh on a score ago. They handed over a piece of cloth tied together holding food and a small coin purse. Gavin knew the risk they took in aiding him.

"'Tis not much," the older of the two proclaimed. "But 'twill help buy a meal or two as you make your way to..." The man's voice trailed off and he shrugged.

"I go to—"

"Nay, my lord," Eben interrupted. "If we know not

where you flee, we cannot give that information to Lord Ashton, should he request it."

The look Eben gave him—and what he left unsaid—convinced Gavin of the wisdom in keeping his plans to himself.

"Then I give you my gratitude, Eben." He looked at the other men gathered about. "To you and to all who have sacrificed for me." He wrapped his arms about Eben, knowing he would never see the older man again. "I'll not forget this day nor your kindness toward me."

He called for Homer. The furball came running from a hiding place and wound through his legs. Gavin lifted the cat and placed him back in his sack. Homer curled up, his brief adventure in the stables over.

He turned and mounted the horse, a nondescript brown. Eben handed up the bundle of clothes. Into a burlap sack hanging from the saddle, Gavin slipped the clothes and the food.

"We'll accompany you to the gates, my lord."

Gavin nodded, words failing him, his throat thick with emotion. They reached the entrance to Ashgrove. Eben himself opened the gate, glaring at the watchmen upon the tower above.

"Godspeed, my lord."

Gavin gave a wave and managed a smile. No matter how heavy his heart, he must put on a good face for the rest of the world.

For the rest of his life.

8

"I'm dying. Let us face that fact before we begin this discussion, eh, Robert?"

Robert found it hard to agree with Lord Aldred. This man had been the hero of his youth. Invincible. Like a god. Yet upon closer study, he noticed how much weight Aldred no longer possessed. Strong muscles had turned to frail arms. His beard, once neatly trimmed, now looked scraggly. A haggard look hung about his features. Still, strength of will and character shone in the warrior's eyes.

He gripped the old warrior's hand. "We all die at some point, my lord. You have lived a long and happy life. Who is to say when 'twill end?"

Aldred glared up at him. "I don't want you to placate me, boy. Just agree with me. I'm dying. My strength ebbs away. I'm uncomfortable in any position I stand, sit, or lie in. My bones ache. My belly seems forever noxious. My breath has turned foul. I'm a man with little time. Agreed?"

Robert bowed his head and then nodded, not able to look at Lord Aldred. When did this change occur? He visited Kentwood every month or so. When had the mighty knight begun to fade away? Why hadn't he noticed? Or better yet, why had he ignored all the signs?

"Fine. Now that we've established that, I have a request to make of you."

He raised his head. The nobleman's eyes bore into his own. A grown man, and he still could tremble from a single glance given by Lord Aldred. "How may I assist you? You know there's nothing I wouldn't do for you, my lord."

"I want you to wed Elizabeth."

"Marry... Elizabeth?" His voice came out a whisper. He swallowed. "Surely, 'tis the king's decision as to what happens to her and Kentwood. Once you are gone."

Aldred snorted. "Edward owes me. He will honor my request. Besides, our two lands could be joined as one. That alone will appeal to our king. We are close to the coast. An invasion by the French is unlikely, but a united property would make for a strong defense.

"Besides," Aldred finished, "you love her. A great deal."

Robert felt a flush of guilt rise in his cheeks. "We are but good friends, my lord. I have never gone behind your back. I have never—will never—touch Elizabeth in a familiar fashion."

Aldred smiled benignly. "I know that. But I've seen you look at her when you thought no one watched. True, you have a special friendship already, and that will make for a firm foundation for your marriage."

The old man cleared his throat. "Elizabeth needs a younger man in her life, one who can give her children. She has so much to give the man she marries. She's been a best friend to me, a boon companion in my old age. She's smart, quick as lightning, and I would have loved to put her up against any one of my knights from years past had she been born a man. I think she might have presented a great challenge. Even to Gavin."

Aldred paused. "I miss that boy. He was one of the bravest soldiers I've seen. Certainly the best that ever fostered at Kentwood under me."

"I miss him, as well," Robert agreed, his heart heavy. "I've not seen him since our imprisonment in France. I sent three missives to his home in the north. The first two received no response. I suppose the messages went astray. Finally, his father answered the third."

"Berwyn?" Aldred snorted in disgust. "That pompous ass never deserved a son as fine as Gavin."

"Lord Ashton wrote to me that Gavin remained in France. I assume he stayed on after his ransom was paid and fights to this day." He swallowed his frustration as he chose his words carefully. "I wish I could be at war again, as well. Yet Father needs me at home more. King Edward insisted I stay here."

Aldred sighed. "Both of us long to be again at war, my son. There's nothing that challenges a man's skills and prowess more than to be thrust onto the battlefield in the face of danger."

The once mighty soldier waved away such thoughts. "We should enjoy our beautiful surroundings, Robert. We lead fine lives here in peace. Remember the cries of anguish? The blood freely spilt? War should be outlawed. If women ruled, it very well would be."

The old knight shivered and pulled the bedclothes more tightly about him. "No talk of this to Elizabeth. I'll not have her worried about me more than she does already. But when the time comes, give her time to mourn me. I'll ask Edward to do the same. In a year's time, even six months, when she adjusts to the idea of being alone, approach her."

"And if she won't have me?" Robert narrowed his eyes. "You know how obstinate she can be."

Aldred smiled. "Then woo her, Robert. Show her your love. Let your kiss arouse things within her that she never dreamed were there."

Suddenly, Aldred's meaning became clear to him. "You mean..."

Aldred nodded. "Elizabeth is yet a virgin. I could not perform my husbandly duties after we wed. She deserves much more. And if she's stubborn, take her. Show her how grand love can be with the right partner in your arms.

"You're a handsome man, Robert, and a good one. Clever, too. I have the utmost faith that you'll win her over."

"She would hate it if she could hear us discussing her in this manner. And despite pretty words and moonlight kisses, I do not know if she would be willing to have me, my lord. I am more brother to her than lover."

"Then I will ask of Edward to give her the year alone to mourn. When 'tis over, if Elizabeth will not marry you of her own free will, Edward will make certain that it happens. She may think she knows what 'tis best for her, my son, but in the end 'tis for men to make these decisions."

He glanced over at the table next to his bedside. Robert followed his gaze.

"See those stewed plums? My pain has passed. I could enjoy a bite or two of those now."

Robert retrieved the bowl. He glanced down at

Aldred's hands, shaking unsteadily, much as his own father's now did.

"Here, let me help you, my lord." With that, he spooned a bite into Aldred's mouth, all the while thinking of Elizabeth.

"Your Majesty?"

Edward raised his eyes to the adviser. "What now?" he asked irritably. "I will not hear 'tis King John again. Had I known how much trouble that man would cause, I would have forbade him entrance and slammed the door in his face."

The councilor glibly replied, "I'm sure the Black Prince will take that into consideration and locate a more cooperative hostage next time, Sire."

He sighed, shaking his head. "Know ye what that French monarch demanded yesterday? Or the day before that?" Edward slammed down a fist. The candle on the table flickered with the movement. "'Tis two years I have put up with the man, yet we are no closer to negotiating his release than the very day of his capture. This much ransom, that many hostages. Sometimes, I wish to lop off his head and return it to the *dauphin*."

"War can be lengthy, Your Majesty, as well as expensive. I would advise you to let King John keep his head for now. He'll be worth more with it attached to his body. Be patient."

"I'm tired of being patient!" he roared. "And why are you here? Do you bring word from my son?"

The councilor replied, "No word from Prince Edward, Your Majesty. Nor from John of Gaunt. 'Tis a messenger, though, that I think you would see."

The king studied his adviser. The man's beady eyes gleamed in anticipation. "Give me the missive," he said cautiously.

"I think 'twould be wise to see this messenger in person."

Edward was intrigued. "Then bring him to me." He wondered what was so important that he must lay eyes on the envoy. His curiosity grew.

Moments later, the courier shuffled in, flustered as so many were in the royal presence. Did they not understand he ate and drank and wenched and belched just like an ordinary man?

"Your Highness." The man bowed low.

"Rise. Bring me your message." He thrust out a hand to receive it. "Are you to wait for a reply?"

"Not necessarily, Your Highness. I was told to wait and see if you felt a reply was necessary." The messenger placed the missive in Edward's hand.

He studied the man, not immediately recognizing the colors he wore. "And you are from?"

"Fondren, Sire. But the message is not from Lord Markham of Fondren. Nay, this comes from Lord Aldred of Kentwood instead."

Edward relaxed and rewarded the messenger with a smile. "Aldred, you say?"

He sat and placed the scroll upon the table, breaking its seal and unrolling it. Aldred brought fond memories indeed. For two score, the nobleman was England's premier knight, his bravery on the battlefield matched by his keen intelligence and wicked sense of humor.

But why not a messenger directly from Kentwood itself? If memory served him correctly, Fondren bordered upon Aldred's own property. Why a roundabout way of communications? Were there French spies at Kentwood?

Edward smoothed the parchment and began to read.

Greetings, my king –

I trust this finds you well and in good spirits. I miss our exploits on the battlefield as much as a nursing babe misses his mother's breast. War has been my calling in life, and I often long for those days of yore, full of splendor and challenge.

Now to business, and I will not resort to flattery, though you know the high esteem I hold for you, my liege. You not only bring England glory every day, but you are a good man, one I admire and respect.

I find I am in the twilight of my years. 'Tis been a good life, one made even more pleasant by my dearest Elizabeth, whom you have met. I worry about her well-being and what will happen to her upon my death. You know of her beauty and wit, her charm and intelligence. I would ask that you grant a last favor to a faithful soldier, as 'tis in your power alone.

As I have no surviving heir, Elizabeth's fate will be up to you upon my death. Give her time to mourn, my king. Do not make her a political pawn and rush her into another union. For all her strength, Elizabeth is yet fragile. I would request you give her in marriage to my neighbor, Sir Robert of Fondren, only son of Lord Markham. Our properties adjoin and could thus be united. Lord Robert is a good man and familiar to her. 'Twould be a most advantageous situation for all.

Think it over, my liege, and remember my years of service to you. I hope you will honor my small request. If you feel need to reply, please direct your missive to Robert at Fondren. I would not worry my most beloved wife about such matters.

As always, your humble servant,
    Lord Aldred of Kentwood

Edward touched the page, running a finger over Aldred's name. The signature, written in a different hand than the letter's contents, was barely recognizable. More than likely, Aldred's health had deteriorated so much that he dictated the letter and then signed his name to it. The seal had been genuine, though, and the tone was so like his old friend. Edward had no doubt the missive came from none other than Lord Aldred.

He remembered Elizabeth's great beauty from previous visits to Kentwood. Her quick wit and vivacity only complimented her striking looks. She would be a great prize for any of his knights upon Aldred's passing. Yet Aldred's proposal made sense. To merge the two adjoining estates would be wise. Sir Robert of Fondren was a proven, dedicated soldier. With his steadfastness and Elizabeth's beauty and intelligence, 'twould result in fine children that would be loyal to the crown.

Edward decided to give Aldred peace of mind and honor this reasonable request. Upon the knight's death, his widow would have sufficient time to grieve before she received word from her king to marry Sir Robert.

He called for ink and clean parchment and wrote a quick response to Aldred before charging the messenger to return the missive to Fondren.

"'Tis for your lord to deliver to Lord Aldred. Take it to no other," he warned as he handed over the freshly-sealed missive.

As the messenger left, Edward found himself in much better spirits. So good, in fact, that he decided he would call upon his prisoner. King John enjoyed visitors, especially those who played chess.

He smiled to himself. The French monarch was abysmal at chess. And Edward was in the mood to win.

As always.

9

"Wife, will you stop fretting over me? I am fine, just stiff from all the time spent in bed. I need to be up and about. I insist that you let me be."

Elizabeth hid her smile from an exasperated Aldred. He'd been up several times in the last few days, practicing on how to get around with his new walking stick of fine mahogany, a gift from Robert.

"Tell me if you are not feeling well or if you are simply overtired. I will return you to your bed, my lord, and make all the proper excuses afterward."

He snorted and leaned upon the stick. "I missed the last judgment day. I look forward to this one. Nothing will keep me from my people today."

"Especially now that the Lenten season has passed? I know how you miss your sweets during fasting." She walked to him and kissed his wrinkled cheek. "Besides, the people knew you suffered from chills and fever. All understood. 'Tis been a dreadful winter these past few months. I am happy spring is finally here."

She walked to the small window, a luxury Aldred

had added to the solar at her request, and gazed out. "The earth turns green again, my lord."

Her husband joined her at the window. He brought an arm about her waist. "I hear you have a new tapestry finished that will keep the blustery spring winds from invading our great hall."

His eyes had their old sparkle back. She breathed a sigh of relief. "Yes, Aldred. I hope 'twill please you. You may even recognize a scene or two from your past adventures woven upon it."

He gave her a squeeze. "You always please me, Elizabeth. You have perfect sense in every way. Whatever changes you have made since I last saw the great hall will no doubt be wise ones. I wonder why I even bother to accompany you to these judgment days. You do so well on your own."

She turned and placed a hand upon his sleeve. "I need you, my husband. I will always need your guidance." She smiled gently at him. "You made me what I am today. I wish to please you in every way. Make you proud of me."

Aldred returned her smile and took her hand. "You will please me by getting me downstairs and settled before the proceedings begin."

"Then take your new stick in hand. Do not rush. And do not think I will miss seeing if you favor your right leg. I will be watching for that. You may have your strength back, but you must—"

"No fussing," he retorted. "No hovering. Simply let me be."

She heard the affection in his voice, despite the gruff words. Sweet Jesu, how this man had become her entire world. She thanked God Almighty at mass every morning for bringing Aldred into her life.

The doubts crept in at night, though, as she lay

next to him, listening to his labored breathing. What would happen to her after his death? Would she finally come face-to face-with her long-awaited date at the nunnery? Or would she be forced to return to her father's castle until the king saw fit to pawn her off onto another nobleman, one that would demand his marital rights?

More importantly, who would receive Kentwood? No one could care for the estate as she had. The property thrived now, in no small part due to her excellent management skills. She'd made Kentwood what it was. She deserved to keep it. Damn the silly rules that would not allow a woman to be awarded an estate upon her husband's death.

Still, no sense in dwelling on the matter. Their people awaited them. Rulings needed to be issued. Disputes must be settled. And afterward, they would feast. She had hired a new troubadour to sing of Aldred's exploits, hoping to cheer him.

Elizabeth swore to enjoy one day at a time. For as many as were left.

———

Gavin approached Kentwood, hoping to make a better impression than he had at Ashgrove. He was still thinner than before his imprisonment, but not as bedraggled as a few months ago. He now wore clothes instead of rags, though their fit left something to be desired.

He was cleaner now, too, things he hadn't thought of as he'd urged his tired body homeward three weeks before. He'd taken time to stop and bathe in the cold waters of a nearby river. With some of the coins that had been given to him, he had purchased a razor and was clean-shaven again. The knots were long gone from his hair, which was neatly trimmed. His fatigue lessened each day and his strength grew as he ate better. Making the long journey on horseback was much easier on his body than his trip from London north to Ashgrove.

He wanted to look the best he possibly could before Lord Aldred. He hadn't seen the warrior in years, not since Crecy over half a score ago. As Kentwood came into his sight, he realized how much he'd missed Aldred and all those at his large estate.

Gavin believed the nobleman would give him a home for now. He would ask to be attached to Lord Aldred's guard, if possible, or even to Robert's household, which he knew lay nearby. Or would Lord Aldred advise Gavin to play the knight-errant, seeking adventure and fortune as he went? He had entertained thoughts of returning to the war in France, if nothing else materialized, though he loathed the thought of being on French soil again.

In his highest hopes, Gavin wished Lord Aldred's connections would allow him a place in King Edward's retinue. He would give his life for his king and had the skills to protect the royal in any circumstance, if Edward would consider making Gavin a part of his royal guard.

His determination to go on, though, drove his every thought, much as it had during his imprisonment in France. Anything would be better than living in that cramped cell with the dying all about him. Their pitiful cries still haunted his dreams.

As Gavin moved closer to his destination, he saw the gates opened wide. He stroked Homer's head absently as he rode on, shaking the nightmare images of the prison cell from his head.

"'Tis judgment day," he told the kitten, who gnawed playfully on his finger.

He climbed from his horse and walked it up to the portal. Gavin spied a now gray-haired Rufus and called out a greeting. The burly soldier hurried over to him, surprise written across his face.

"Captain of the guard, Sir Rufus," he said, recognizing the insignia Rufus wore. "I am impressed with your accomplishments."

Rufus slapped him on the back. "Why if 'tis not Sir Gavin. Come home from the wars in France, I dare say."

He pumped Gavin's hand enthusiastically as he studied him. Gavin saw the look of concern flicker across the soldier's features.

"And how are you, old friend? Was the fighting so terrible? 'Tis reed-thin and pale you are, my lord."

"I've been better, Rufus, but 'tis good to be home on English soil once more."

The soldier smiled broadly. "I still remember you as a lad at Crecy. You showed such bravery. Oh, my Lord Aldred will be happy to see you at his table tonight. 'Tis like the Prodigal Son, returning home to Kentwood again."

He laughed. "But I am neither son nor have I misspent my youth, Captain."

"Nevertheless, his lordship would want a fatted calf killed in your honor if a feast 'tweren't already planned."

Gavin cocked his head. "And what celebration occurs today?"

"'Tis custom, sir. Lady Elizabeth started it. After each judgment day, all are welcome for a bountiful meal with dancing and music. My lady is wonderful, well-loved by all. You will see what I mean. Kentwood 'twould not be the same without her."

Rufus motioned him forward. "Come. I will escort you to the great hall myself." He signaled for Gavin's horse to be taken and cared for.

He followed the knight into Kentwood. The great hall teemed with people. Rufus bowed and left to return to his post, wishing Gavin well. He surveyed the room for Lord Aldred even as Rufus left.

He spied his former overlord on the dais, but the sight took him aback. An old man wearing Lord Aldred's visage and clothes sat upon the platform. His posture caused him to stoop in his chair. A shag of white hair now replaced the salt and pepper of Gavin's memory. In the ten years since he'd last seen him, Lord Aldred had aged considerably.

His eyes wandered to the woman seated to Aldred's right. Even at this distance, he saw how comely she was. A gorgeous mass of auburn curls spilled down the back of her dark blue surcoat. 'Twas almost a sinful display of great beauty, to have hair unbound in such a manner. She sat as royalty would, with a self-assurance and grace that made her all the more attractive.

Every now and then, she turned to Lord Aldred and chatted easily. The camaraderie between them was obvious. Gavin listened as she rendered several judgments in a row. He realized this woman had become the real power at Kentwood. Immediately, resentment festered in him. For Lord Aldred to age was one thing. For him to lose his authority to a woman— albeit his wife—was quite another.

At least her rulings seemed fairly received. She thought quickly in any given situation. Gavin couldn't help but be impressed with her common

sense and easy manner. He almost experienced jealousy at her quick, thoughtful decisions. That skill
would make her a formidable opponent in war. He
was glad she was a woman, for he would never willingly tangle with the likes of her on the battlefield.

"Have we reached all decisions needed on this
day?" Her voice rang out clearly through the hall. He
admired her presence and wondered who her
sire was.

When no one stepped forward, she again called
out, "Does any man or woman wish to speak to Lord
Aldred or myself before we adjourn?"

A half-dozen stepped forward, most praising Lady
Elizabeth in one way or another. It irritated Gavin by
this point at how this lady seemed more revered than
the very master of Kentwood. Finally, he moved toward the dais.

As he stepped up, the last remaining man to
speak, he looked to Lord Aldred.

"I come to pay homage to——"

"Gavin!" Lord Aldred cried in delight. He stood
and then staggered forward.

Gavin rushed toward him and caught the old man
as he fell. He placed the nobleman's still form on the
ground. As he did, he felt the woman's gaze burning
into him.

"My lady," he said, his tone even.

With fire in her green eyes, she almost growled at
him, "If you've killed him, I'll see you dead."

10

Elizabeth rushed to Aldred's side, shoving aside the dark-haired stranger. Panic rose in her. Her heart skipped several beats. Had the day she dreaded finally arrived? Was Aldred dead?

She bent and pressed her cheek against her husband's. "He still breathes," she murmured, reassuring herself. "He has but lost consciousness." She cradled Aldred's head upon her lap, forcing herself to take a calming breath.

When she looked up, her eyes met the gaze of the outsider's. Fresh anger simmered through her again.

"Lord Aldred has nerves of steel. What manner of man are you that he would faint dead away at the sight of you?" Her voice echoed in the now silent hall as those gathered stood by wordlessly.

She glared at the man, studying him as she would any enemy. He was taller and had broader shoulders than her husband, but he was gaunt and pale, as if someone had locked him away, trying to starve him into submission. That would not be possible, she thought, as she took in his strong jaw now locked firmly in place. She guessed him as stubborn as Aldred had been in his younger days, mayhap more so. Unruly, jet-black hair framed a clean-shaven face. His clothes had seen better days, and on a smaller man, at that.

It was his eyes that drew her in, though. They were very like Aldred's, a warm brown rimmed in amber. They even had flecks of green in them, as Aldred's did when he was angry. Those eyes challenged her now. She wondered what relative this must be. She knew of no kin Aldred claimed, yet this man favored him.

Elizabeth sensed the outsider came for Kentwood. Would he be its new heir? Her heart ached at the thought of losing her home to this stranger, yet if 'twere the case, he looked most capable.

She looked up at the man who knelt beside her, waiting for his reply. Before he answered, a faint yowl sounded. Then a head of fur popped out from a sack worn about the stranger's neck.

A kitten looked about the room and scurried from its resting place. It landed next to Aldred and studied him for a moment before a quick, pink tongue grazed the nobleman's cheek.

Aldred wrinkled his nose and sneezed. The kitten jumped a good foot in the air and scrambled back up into his owner's lap, looking over its shoulder as Aldred stirred.

"My lord?" Elizabeth said softly.

Aldred opened his eyes and smiled up at her. "Hello, dearest."

She stroked his cheek. "Do you feel you can sit up?"

He frowned. "I had the most unusual vision. I thought for a moment I saw Sir Gavin of Ashgrove standing before me."

"You did, my lord," the dark stranger spoke up. "I have come to visit you and your wife." He looked at Elizabeth as if she would challenge his words.

Aldred pushed himself up. She heard a collective sigh released from those gathered in the room. Suddenly, she was aware of every eye in the great hall upon them.

"Let us get you to bed, my lord." She slipped a hand under his arm. The stranger did the same on the opposite side and helped her raise Aldred to his feet.

"Not to bed, my lady," chided her husband. "I simply fainted away, so surprised was I at seeing Gavin after so many years."

Gavin.

"Yes, my lord. I've heard you speak of Sir Gavin." Elizabeth looked questioningly at the handsome newcomer. "So nice of you to visit. Unannounced." Wrath still blazed through her at the stress this uninvited guest had placed upon her husband.

The knight shrugged, not rising to the bait she cast out.

Aldred motioned for his walking stick. "Come, join us as we celebrate another fruitful month at Kentwood," he told Gavin. Then turning, he raised his voice to those in the room. "Let our festivities begin," he called out. "Sir Gavin shall be our honored guest."

The crowd murmured in assent, their mood reflecting their master's positive tone.

"You are certain, my lord?"

Gavin watched Lord Aldred's wife as she studied her husband. Concern was written across her brow. From that one look, it reassured him that despite Aldred's poor health, the nobleman had someone who genuinely cared to watch over him.

"Go ahead, Elizabeth. Do what you must to prepare for our celebration." He looked to Gavin. "You can trust Gavin to take good care of me, I'll wager."

"Indeed, my lord," Gavin nodded in agreement. "I am your most humble servant."

Elizabeth gave a curt nod and ventured off. He helped Aldred back into his seat.

"Gavin!"

He turned and saw Robert making his way toward him. He grinned and went to meet his friend. They fell into each other's arms in a tight embrace, laughing at the good fortune of seeing one another again.

"What brings you to Kentwood?" Robert asked, looking him over. "And 'tis but skin and bones you are, looking more like a disreputable commoner than a knight of the realm. Where have you been these last two years?"

"'Tis a long story, my friend. Much has happened since we last spoke. I'll need a cup of strong wine and a few hours to tell the tale."

He motioned Robert to return to the dais with him, where his friend greeted Lord Aldred.

"Good to see you up and about, my lord. I'm sure 'tis a clucking hen Elizabeth has been over you."

Lord Aldred raised the walking stick in his hand. "And my thanks to you, Robert. This new walking stick was just what I needed. If Elizabeth becomes too dictatorial, I shall conk her on the head with it—and then run like the Devil."

Both men laughed at his words. "I'd pay good money to see that, my lord," Robert said. He turned back to Gavin. "Have you met Elizabeth yet?"

"Just for a moment," he replied.

His eyes skimmed the great hall, finding her.

Gavin saw how she assured the people. How self-possessed she was. The lady was in total control of the room, giving orders to clear space, commanding musicians to play while trestle tables were being set up.

The men spoke for a few minutes before she returned to greet Robert and fuss over Aldred again. Gavin saw how much she cared for the old man. A pang of jealousy shot through him. He had no one left to care so for him, now that his beloved mother was dead. It still brought him pain that he had not been able to say goodbye to her, much less even see her grave.

"Would you care to be seated, Sir Gavin?"

Lady Aldred's voice, polite yet cool, brought him from his reverie. He glanced about, seeing things well in place for the feast about to begin.

"Of course," he answered. "I thank you for so graciously inviting me to your banquet."

"If my husband is happy to see you," she said carefully, "then so am I. Please, sit here. Share a trencher with him. I'm sure you have much to speak about to one another."

She indicated her place beside her husband. He tried to protest, but Robert cut him off.

"Give into her, Gavin. 'Tis much easier and takes far less time than fighting with her. Elizabeth always gets her way. Besides," he grinned, "that means she'll share her trencher with me. I know she'll eat far less than you would if we were to be paired together. I might actually have a fighting chance to gobble up most of the many delicacies without coming to blows."

Gavin inclined his head to Elizabeth and took the seat next to Aldred, glad that his good ear faced his friend. A serving maid placed a trencher before them, and Gavin sliced it in two, giving Aldred his half. A chaplain appeared to bless the meal, followed by the steward and his staff, pouring out the wine mixed with honey and ale.

Then the feasting began in earnest. He thought back to the days of celebration in his youth when he fostered at Kentwood. This meal rivaled any from the past. Stork and peacock, then haddock and cod, were followed by venison, mutton, and pork. Those were followed by more pastries than he'd imagined while imprisoned in France, making their way to the trestle tables.

Throughout the meal, though, Aldred ate sparingly of the small, bite-sized pieces placed before him. Gavin watched the old knight closely. The nobleman seemed in good spirits and spoke with true happiness shining from his eyes, helping his guest to relax somewhat. Gavin made the decision not to bring up his recent troubles tonight. There would be plenty of time to speak of those to Lord Aldred on the morrow and seek the old lord's advice.

By the sweets course, Gavin's stomach protested at the great amount he'd already consumed. He hadn't eaten so much at one sitting since he'd last left England. His parents had held a banquet in his honor that night. It all seemed so long ago.

"Cheese, my lord? Or mayhap you would prefer a small cake? Our cook bakes the finest sweets in the land."

He turned to Lady Aldred. "You are a charming hostess, my lady, but I must pass. I fear I have eaten far more than my share."

Robert laughed. "From the looks of it, you haven't

eaten quite enough, Gavin. In truth, you are thin as a stork's leg. Let our Elizabeth fatten you up."

She eyed him with interest. "If you'd like, I can have a tray of assorted goods sent to your bedchamber. That way if you wish to try some later, they would be available to you."

"You are most gracious, my lady."

"My lord," Robert addressed Aldred, "might I steal Gavin away from you for a few minutes before the song begins? I would love to converse with my old friend."

Aldred snorted. "More than likely you seek to point out all the beautiful, unattached women in the room, Robert." He stood. "I think I shall retire, so you are welcomed to speak to Gavin to your heart's content."

Lady Aldred joined her husband. "Are you very tired, my lord?" A shadow crossed her face. "I so wanted you to hear this new troubadour sing your praises."

Lord Aldred cupped her cheek with his hand. "Mayhap another time, Elizabeth. I am certain you engaged him for a fortnight or longer."

She blushed a pretty pink. "I may have, now that you mention it. But let me see you settled."

Her husband held out a hand to her. "Nay. Simon will see to my needs. Stay and entertain our guests." He signaled the servant over. "Good eve to you, gentlemen. I look forward to speaking more to you on the morrow, Gavin. I am afraid I talked your ear off tonight."

Gavin bowed. "'Twas talk I was so inclined to hear, my lord. I thank you for sheltering me for the night."

Lord Aldred clasped his hand. "For this night and as long as you wish to stay, my boy. You are always welcome at Kentwood. Simon?"

"My lord?" The servant stepped up and allowed Aldred to lean upon him. Gavin was drawn to watching Lady Aldred as she herself watched her husband escorted from the room.

"I must excuse myself," she said. "I would speak to the troubadour. He sings tonight of Lord Aldred and his many victories in battle. I would have that saved for another time when my lord husband can hear and enjoy."

She curtsied to them and moved across the room. He followed her progress as she stopped and talked to one group then the next. She seemed to know everyone by name and exhibit a genuine care for all.

Soon the strains of a psalterian began. He caught sight of the singer as he brought the zither close to his chest and began plucking at its strings. The troubadour sang of the glory of England and of both King Edward's and the Black Prince's mastery over France. Robert must have sensed Gavin was in no mood to speak seriously, for he kept their conversation light.

Then the troubadour began to sing of Lady Aldred, weaving tales of her generosity and kind spirit.

"Men compose songs about her?" he asked Robert.

"Of course. Elizabeth is a celebrated beauty of some renown in these parts. She numbers even King Edward as a devoted follower. He claims to enjoy visiting Kentwood more for Elizabeth's company than Lord Aldred's." Robert chuckled.

"And how long have she and Lord Aldred been married?"

Robert thought a moment. "'Tis been a good one-

and-ten years, I think, since she came to Kentwood to wed. Her sire brought her himself. Lord Bramwell of Aldwyn. I gather she was quite a handful as a child, and he escorted her here so that there would be no chance of her running away."

"But her beauty and dowry overcame those short-comings?" he asked. "As if Lord Aldred needed her money."

Robert grew quiet. "There was a time the dowry price came in handy, Gavin. Things were not flourishing at Kentwood after we returned from Crecy."

"Was it plague?"

"Nay, not for a while. It did rage in London and finally arrived in the south, but I speak of other things. Harvests gone bad. Tenants mishandled during Lord Aldred's lengthy absence. Almost an indifference that had cropped up in the years Lord Aldred spent at war."

"I see he's turned it around, though. Leave it to Lord Aldred to manage in a crisis." He reached for his honeyed wine.

"Nay, 'twas not his doing. 'Twas all Elizabeth's."

He froze in mid-air, his cup not yet to his lips. "Lady Aldred? A woman? Surely, things were not as bad as you make them seem, my friend." He took a swig from the silver goblet.

"You are wrong, Gavin. Where servants were list-less and inactive, Elizabeth swept them into action. She visited tenants and had roofs repaired. Went into the fields and talked to the peasants about the best ways to grow crops. She did a thousand things, both large and small, to get Kentwood back on track."

He followed Robert's gaze as his good friend spoke Lady Aldred's praises. It lay on the lady herself.

"There is nothing she cannot do, Gavin. Nothing."

"You seem to admire her quite a bit."

Robert flushed. In that moment, Gavin realized his friend had deep feelings.

For another man's wife.

11

Aldred awakened, refreshed by his night's restful sleep. He was glad the cold had started to recede, though his old bones never seemed to warm completely anymore. At least spring would soon make her annual appearance. He wondered idly if he would be here to see spring's birth this time next year and decided he would not. His time on earth drew near. Yet he was fortunate. He had lived the life he'd wished to, on his own terms, and he wouldn't change a thing about it. He would end his days happily, spending what little time remained with those he loved.

And how he loved Elizabeth. She would be by shortly, having attended mass, broken her fast, and issued orders for the day to their staff. Pride filled him at all she accomplished on a daily basis, far more than any woman of his acquaintance. Theirs was not a physical love, one of grand passion. No, it favored affection, tender feelings, and goodwill. She was friend, daughter, and wife all captured in one.

He hoped arranging for her betrothal to Robert would please her after he was gone. Robert was a good man, and he was more than a little fond of Elizabeth, despite his protests to the contrary.

Aldred pushed himself up, propping pillows behind his back and smoothing his hair. He looked forward to a visit from Gavin this morning. The boy worried him, a former shell of the man he'd been when Aldred last saw him. Obviously, the war in France had not been kind to Gavin Garwood.

He was troubled, too. Aldred sensed it in Gavin's wary gaze, in the cock of his head. If not the war, 'twould mean only one thing amiss.

Berwyn.

Aldred cursed the day Berwyn arrived upon his property. Physically gifted, he was a good soldier—when he bothered to listen. He had peas for brains, though. A good estate manager and sweet wife, along with years of decent weather, had allowed Berwyn's estate to prosper.

What bothered Aldred was the man's loose morals. He found neither honor nor loyalty in the boy who had become Lord Ashton. Oh, the nobleman was sure he said the right things when certain ears were present, yet he was quick to speak ill of someone the minute that man's back was turned. Only as a favor to Gillian had Aldred decided to foster Gavin, hoping his influence on the boy might override that of his worthless father.

That proved to be a blessing in disguise. Gavin's talents were limitless. Skilled at war games and a keen hunter, the young boy also showed unswerving fidelity to his liege lord and his friends. Guilt racked Aldred when Gavin had fostered at Kentwood because he'd grown to love the boy more than his own kin.

A knock sounded at the door, and Elizabeth poked

in her head. She smiled as she brought him a tray of food.

"I trust you had a good night, my lord?"

She opened all sides of the bed curtains and put the tray in his lap before going to feed fresh wood into the fire.

He immediately felt the warmth of the fire's blaze and sighed in contentment. "Did you know you please me in every way, Wife?" he asked.

She laughed. "I would love to record your words, Aldred, for I fear you are most forgetful. I remember times when you have cautioned me for being too headstrong, too stubborn, blind to the—"

"Enough," he protested, cutting her off as he pulled a piece of bread apart. "Mayhap there has been a time or two that you distressed me. Overall, though, you are tolerable, I suppose." He grinned mischievously at her.

A knock at the open door interrupted their playful banter. He looked up and saw Gavin standing there hesitantly.

"Come in, Gavin, come in. I hope all is well? You are pleased with your bedchamber? The bed itself?"

"Yes, my lord. Though I would have been happy with a pallet on the floor of the great hall, the luxury of having a chamber to myself has me feeling as if I were royalty. Everything is most splendid."

Aldred watched Gavin step through the portal. He eyed Elizabeth uncertainly, and then turned his attention back to Aldred.

For his part, Aldred was amused. Elizabeth intimidated many a man. For all her youth and beauty, her air was competent, letting all know that she was quite in charge of things. He sensed Gavin had discovered this and didn't know what to make of her just yet.

"Come closer, Gavin. Closer," he instructed. "I can't hear quite as well as I once did."

"At least that's what he claims," Elizabeth chimed in. "Although this hearing loss only seems to come about whenever I ask him to do something he wishes to avoid."

Aldred chuckled. "She has found me out," he whispered in Gavin's direction before taking his wife's hand and smiling benignly at her.

She dropped his hand. "You, my lord, are impossible. Now break your fast and stop all this quibbling. I have much work to do."

Elizabeth turned to Gavin. "See that he eats, and please do not tire him." She gave a mock glare to Aldred and left the room.

"See what I must put up with?" he asked and sighed. "Now pull up a chair, Gavin. We have much to discuss."

"As long as you eat what 'tis before you," Gavin said as he brought a chair beside the bed. "I would not want your wife to think less of me than she already does."

"Elizabeth? Oh, she'll adore you once she gets to know you. You did not meet under ideal circumstances. She is rather like a mama bear protecting her fragile cub, as far as I am concerned. But 'tis neither here nor there."

He picked up a slice of cheese to nibble on. "So now, my friend. What brings you to Kentwood? Your countenance is a troubled one. You are as thin as a lad of four-and-ten. What ails you, Gavin? 'Tis it the war in France? Or has that father of yours been up to no good?"

Gavin visibly shuddered at the mention of his father's name. That was interesting. It seemed Aldred had been right in thinking this unease that sat upon the lad's shoulders had to do with that fool Berwyn.

The knight raked his hands through his hair, frustrated at where to begin. He sat back in his chair and fidgeted as a boy might. Then the little cat that seemed to be a part of him peeked its head from within the sack it rode in. It used its claws to scamper up Gavin's chest and placed both paws on its master's shoulders.

Aldred heard a loud purr as the creature licked Gavin's chin and proceeded to bump its nose against Gavin's own nose. With a fond smile, he unhooked the cat's claws from his clothing and settled the gray furball in his lap, stroking it as he began to speak.

"I've come to you in need of a favor, my lord," he began.

"'Tis yours to ask, Gavin. You must know I shall grant you anything within my power."

"I am at a crossroads in my life. War no longer appeals to me." A dark shadow crossed his face. Aldred's stomach tightened in response.

"What happened in France, my boy?" he asked softly.

Gavin recounted his and Robert's capture and their first weeks in confinement. Aldred had heard all this before from Robert himself but chose to keep silent, wishing to hear the tale from Gavin's perspective. Nothing varied from the account Robert gave when he returned from being ransomed.

"And after Robert left?" Aldred prodded. "I know word reached Baywith first, and he immediately sent the ransom for his son's release. How long before the French received your father's response?"

Gavin's face grew colorless as he spoke. "A little over a fortnight after Robert's release, I received a brief missive with my... with Lord Ashton's seal upon it. In it, he refused to pay the ransom. He wrote..."

Gavin's voice faltered, and he rested his head in his hands. The cat jumped to the floor and curled up at its master's feet. Aldred waited, knowing what Gavin would say must be painful indeed.

"It said to do with the prisoner as they liked." His head rose, and he met Aldred's eyes with all the bleakness of a frigid winter's day.

Yet the shock of his words weren't nearly as strong as what Aldred saw in an instant. He'd never been one for vanity, and rarely gave his looks a second thought for a majority of his life. He did know women often spent time fussing over their appearance so he'd gifted Elizabeth with a mirror, which seemed to please her.

But he himself eventually became fascinated with the image it displayed. As time passed, he looked often into this mirror, studying what he saw before him. He wondered why men followed him, did whatever he asked without question. He'd wanted to see what was in his face that would cause a man to place himself in peril at the mere request of another man.

And now he knew.

The eyes alone would give it away if no other feature did. Gavin's eyes were his own, a deep brown edged in amber. 'Twere eyes he'd never seen in another, only in the mirror, and now in Gavin himself. His frame, the sensual lips, the very shape of the fingers on his hands—all told the tale.

Aldred cursed himself silently. Why had he not realized it years ago when the boy had fostered under him? He had lived under this very roof for so long. No wonder they had always gotten along so well. Gavin was *his son*. A mistake he'd made long ago, comforting a troubled young girl, now came back to haunt him.

That girl hadn't wished to marry Berwyn. Aldred could well understand why. The solace he sought to give her turned into something much, much more, and for seven magical nights they coupled, loving purely and sweetly before her wedding.

The result of their lovemaking now sat before him. Gavin was the fruit of his and Gillian's brief time spent together. Aldred never dreamed that a child had been made. He had never seen himself in the young boy that came to foster with him so many years ago.

And now that boy was a man, lost and alone, disavowed by the man who had raised him as his own flesh and blood.

He amazed himself by finding his voice. "Did you suffer much?"

"Aye." The word came out softly and hung in the air. Gavin drew in a long breath and exhaled it slowly. "'Twas two years at the hands of those French bastards. Two long, long years. Spent in fear and loneliness and pain. I have scars on my back that will never heal. I lost the hearing in my left ear."

He stood now and began to pace the solar as he continued his tale, the cat following on his heels. "I escaped through the help of a dying priest and made my way home. Home," he repeated softly, and Aldred heard the bitterness in Gavin's voice.

"How did Berwyn explain his actions to you?"

Gavin spun around. "With a sword pointed at my heart and his new wife, who is with child, looking on. He told me my mother had been a whore and that I was not of his blood." A tear coursed down Gavin's cheek. "I hadn't even known she had passed away," he whispered. "What kept me going was knowing how much she loved me. And I never had a chance to say goodbye."

He brought himself up to his full height and returned to his chair. The cat sprang into his lap and curled into a ball. "I do not wish your pity, my lord. Far from it. I wish simply to be useful. To learn to make my way in the world without land or fortune."

Gavin's mouth turned down. "I find I have no taste for war, so I no longer wish to return to France. That could change, of course. 'Tis not fear of battle I find within me, only a loathing to return to French soil so quickly."

Aldred composed himself. "I well understand that, Gavin. How may I aid you?"

His son looked Aldred squarely in the eye. "I would ask that you allow me to serve in your guard. I would consider it an honor. If you have no room for me, I would gladly ask the same of Robert's father, though I have never met him.

"Or," Gavin continued, a steely determination coming over him, "I know that you have the ear of King Edward. If you think there's an inkling of a chance for me to be of service to the king in his royal guard, I would be most grateful if you could request an audience for me to plead my case."

Aldred's heart grew heavy. His own flesh and blood had suffered so, first at the hands of the French and then Berwyn. He wanted to run a sword through the man, so great was his anger at Berwyn's betrayal of Gavin. Yet he must keep his head.

"I would be selfish, Gavin, and ask that you stay here as captain of my guard until my death. 'Twill be before the year is out, I suppose, despite all Elizabeth's ministrations. I most certainly will send word to King Edward, however, and after I am gone, I'm sure your situation will fast improve."

Aldred decided to write the king that very day. He now had a worthy heir to Kentwood.

And a husband for his Elizabeth.

12

Aldred thought carefully as he composed each line of the letter to Edward. Though he had the utmost respect for his monarch, the king threw constant, heated tantrums, much as a small child who didn't get a treat. He did not want a single word to offend the ruler, thus ruining his case for Gavin inheriting Kentwood.

He had spent most of the morning weighing the decision. The conclusion seemed obvious. Neither Elizabeth nor Gavin would be told of his plans. If he worded his request well, he knew in his heart Edward would grant it, if only to reward Aldred's long years of service to the crown.

Most importantly, Aldred hoped it would cause no bitterness between Gavin and Robert—but it was a chance he was willing to risk. His promise to Robert of Elizabeth's hand in marriage after his death had been sincere, but the circumstances had changed so rapidly. They altered the decision Aldred had made before.

As much as he enjoyed Robert's company and thought well of the knight, Aldred knew Elizabeth and Kentwood must be for Gavin. His son was the one man who could be her true equal. He would match Elizabeth in both wit and intelligence. Gavin would provide her with the challenges she so dearly loved. His son also had a sweetness of spirit about him, which would do well for Elizabeth, especially since she would be coming to their marital bed as a virgin.

More importantly, Elizabeth would remain at Kentwood. She loved the place as much as Aldred himself. She saw to its day-to-day running and planned well in advance for every foreseeable problem down the road. She would relish remaining at her home, albeit it in a diminished capacity. If Gavin were as intelligent as Aldred gave him credit for, he'd make good use of the knowledge Elizabeth had accumulated in the last decade residing at Kentwood. If not, he would be making a mistake. Aldred saw it a correctable one. He trusted Elizabeth had enough love in her heart for Kentwood and a good man, once she was placed in that position.

A tap on the door caused him to turn in that direction. The simple movement brought a pain to his side.

"Come." He put on a cheerful countenance as his wife sailed through the portal.

She stopped in her tracks. "Might I ask why you are not resting? And why you are attempting to write something? You know how easily you tire, Husband, and how your eyesight is strained when you read."

He smiled and motioned for her to come closer as he signed his work of the past hour. "'Tis a missive I write to King Edward." He folded the parchment and drizzled wax upon it, grateful she hadn't seen its contents.

Elizabeth placed a hand upon his shoulder. "I have aided you with correspondence many times.

Cedd has done so, as well. Can we not make ourselves useful?"

She reached for his signet ring from where it sat upon the table and pressed it into the warm wax.

"I thought 'twas best that it came from me personally. 'Twas a delicate matter I addressed. I wanted it in my own hand. Small things such as that mean a great deal to our king."

She studied him a moment. "Does it concern Sir Gavin?"

He nodded. "He mentioned that he would like to serve in the king's royal guard. I felt a personal recommendation was just the right touch in bringing the king's attention to Gavin's unfortunate circumstance."

A small lie, though Gavin had mentioned serving in the king's guard. It troubled Aldred that he lied to his wife, something he had never done previously. Still, he wanted to hear from Edward first before he revealed his plans to Elizabeth regarding her future.

"Well, I don't like him," she declared. "He comes out of nowhere, gives you the fright of your life, and has monopolized your time since he's been here." She clucked her tongue in disapproval.

"Now, now. Give the boy a chance. 'Tis good character he possesses, as well as being a fine warrior, and a most crushing blow he has been dealt."

Aldred explained briefly about Gavin's imprisonment in France and how his father refused to ransom him, leading to his miserable confinement for two years in a squalid prison.

"To make matters worse, after he managed to escape, Gavin made his way home to Ashgrove, which lies near the border of England and Scotland, only to find his dearest mother dead and his father remarried to one of his young mistresses." Aldred added, "Berwyn claimed that he'd learned Gavin was not of his blood. That his wife had deceived him for all these years."

Elizabeth's eyes filled with tears. "What an awful thing to learn, especially after barely surviving for two years in such dismal conditions."

"It means that Gavin no longer will inherit Ashgrove. He is no longer welcomed there. Berwyn's new wife is already with child, and 'twill be her babe that acquires Ashgrove one day."

Aldred took his wife's hand. "So you see, my dearest, Gavin literally has no home, no funds, and nowhere to go. He came to me for advice. I would do right by him. He is the bravest, most capable knight who ever fostered under me. He shall be captain of my guard once he is well and serve me until the Most Holy Father sees fit to bring me home."

"You will not see Heaven for many a year, Husband." She sighed testily. "I suppose we are stuck with Sir Gavin for a good while."

He laughed. "Be that as it may. Still, I would ask that you keep what I have revealed to you in confidence. Not even Robert yet knows of what Gavin suffered."

Her eyes widened. "Oh, you know Robert. 'Twill be guilt that runs through him once he discovers he left his closest friend behind to a fate worse than death."

"Which is why this must stay between the two of us, my dear. I know not what Gavin intends to share with Robert."

She nodded. "Agreed. Now let us get you abed and rested so you can enjoy the festivities tonight. We had no dancing once you retired last night. The troubadour held his tale of your greatness. If you are up to it, the people would appreciate you coming down again for this celebration."

"Then 'tis a nap for me. To think I started out my life as a babe, napping my days away. Who knew 'twould be the way of the elderly, too?"

———

Elizabeth left Aldred asleep on the bed and closed the door to the solar behind her. She thought to check on their guest at present. He'd not appeared for the noon meal and had requested a tray in his room instead. After what she had learned from Aldred, she had more sympathy for Sir Gavin.

Why, he seemed almost like a woman in his present position, with no control over his fortunes. He was wise to turn to Aldred for advice in such a time of personal crisis. If he were as capable as Aldred led her to believe, she was certain King Edward would want him as a member of the royal guard. His reputation as a master soldier must proceed him, at any rate. Aldred praised few men, and this Sir Gavin won high praise from her husband.

It haunted her, though, that the knight so favored Aldred. Yet her husband gave nary a mention to Gavin being close kin, much less a son to him. He merely shared fond memories and held a great affection for the man whom he'd fostered from a small boy. Besides, she was certain Aldred would have acknowledged Sir Gavin if he were a true blood relative, especially in light of Sir Gavin's current predicament.

Should she share her thoughts with her husband? Or with Robert?

No, best to keep these feelings to herself. She was

misreading the situation. The two men might share a resemblance in their eyes and their builds, but their coloring was very different. And Gavin's hair was black as night. Elizabeth knew Aldred's to have been quite fair before it turned to white in his old age.

She would keep such silly notions to herself.

Elizabeth walked down the stone corridor. Flickering shadows from the sconces danced against the walls. She reached the bedchamber she'd directed the servants to take their guest to last evening and knocked lightly. When no reply came, she became concerned. She decided to open the door and look inside, to be sure nothing was amiss.

The knight lay on the bed, his hands pillowed behind his head, staring at the ceiling, his cat curled up in a ball against his leg. A single candle burned next to the bed. Her earlier feelings of anger toward their guest began to thaw. Animals were supposed to be a good judge of character. If so, Sir Gavin must have a soft spot, for his cat snuggled against him, purring away in total trust.

She found sympathy rising within her for the troubles he had faced. Knowing his circumstances influenced this new feeling. Had she judged too harshly and too soon? Rarely was she guilty of either. He certainly didn't look as fierce as she remembered, either. Instead, she now noticed how handsome he was, more so than any of the many suitors her father had paraded before her so many years ago. She swore to herself that she would put aside her first impressions of the man and start anew.

She wondered if she should knock again in order to gain his attention or merely leave.

Before she could act, he called out to her. "Please. Come in, my lady."

She did so. His face turned toward her, those eyes burning into her with an intensity that Aldred's never possessed as she approached him.

"I thank you for the use of this bedchamber. And the bed. And the wash basin." He sat up, placing his hands upon his knees. "I can't tell you what a luxury sleeping in a bed is. May you never go to war, my lady."

Or to prison, her thoughts echoed. She would keep the secrets Aldred shared with her.

Elizabeth studied their guest a moment. "I hear you are to serve as captain of my husband's guard. That is quite an honor."

A shadow darkened his face. "'Tis not a position I seek. I know Rufus. He is a good man and excellent soldier. I am most unhappy to replace him, but Lord Aldred thought 'twas best."

She smiled. "'Twill give Rufus a chance to go to the wars in France. He's been eager to do so, but my lord husband would not release him with the men he previously sent to the fight. Your arrival will provide the opportunity Rufus has longed for. Once you are fit, that is. I know Lord Aldred wants you to regain your strength after your time at war in France."

Gavin returned her smile. "Lord Aldred can be most persuasive. I had even thought of going to Fondren and asking to serve there. Lord Aldred assured me that remaining at Kentwood would be in my best interest."

"His heart would break if you left now. 'Tis true happiness filling him since you have returned, Sir Gavin. We both insist that you stay. Once you have regained your strength, you will be happy at the head of Aldred's detail. And in the meantime, he will be able to enjoy your company. 'Twill be good for you both."

She saw the surprise on his face and knew it was because her tone and attitude toward him had changed.

He started to answer her, but she cut him off. "Shall we come to an understanding, my lord? I will welcome your presence in my home. Once my husband is dead, however, you will be free to leave Kentwood if you so desire.

"But until that day," she added, "I will do whatever is in my power to keep my beloved husband happy." A mischievous grin settled upon her face. "If that means I must personally hog-tie you, I shall, but we do want you to remain at Kentwood."

The knight laughed. "I have never had a more convincing offer, my lady." He reached out and took her hand and pressed a courtly kiss upon her knuckles.

13

Gavin entered the merry atmosphere of Kentwood's great hall. Without thinking, he immediately looked for Lady Aldred. No other maid caught his eye, for none had the stream of auburn curls she did.

Just the thought of her brought heat to his hand, the one he'd used to capture hers with in a gentlemanly kiss. How was he to know the effect she would have upon him?

Surely, she'd felt it, too, the jolt, that sudden warmth radiating fire between them. Yet she'd smoothly removed her hand as if nothing were amiss. Oh, she was a cool one.

And that only fanned the fire burning inside him even more.

He spent the remainder of the afternoon after their unsettling encounter outside, walking around the castle, making new acquaintances, and renewing old friendships. Everywhere he went, though, every mouth praised Lady Aldred. She sounded too good to be a flesh and blood woman.

He hoped fervently that she made Lord Aldred happy. Gavin sensed that was the case. Guilt over his sudden lust for his respected elder's wife did not make him happy, however. He had never coveted another man's woman. He'd never had to. His good looks and smooth conversation always won him the hearts of willing female companions. With no experience in stepping aside for another man, he was hard pressed to do so now.

Yet he must. Lord Aldred was like a sire to him. He would not jeopardize their relationship of many years. Nor would he wish to upset Robert, who seemed to have deep feelings for the woman, as well.

Yet he would give a year's time to kiss her but once.

Gavin watched as three children ran past him, a very quick boy and two giggling girls who gave chase. He wondered why Lady Aldred had no children by Aldred. With both his sons dead, Kentwood would revert to the crown upon his death. King Edward could then award the title and estate to any subject he saw fit. It most likely would be one who had pleased him in England's war against France, especially if the Black Prince recommended the man to his father.

Would Robert seek the king's permission to marry Lady Aldred upon her husband's death? Would the king have someone else in mind for the auburn-haired noblewoman? King Edward could bestow Kentwood and Lady Aldred together upon a much-favored knight. The monarch might also give the estate to a nobleman he'd grown partial to, and Lady Aldred to appease another. Her great beauty alone would cause many a man to vie for her hand once news of Lord Aldred's eventual death became common knowledge.

Or would the sovereign make her his mistress? He

was said to favor Lady Aldred, but Gavin could not see her in this role. The king might appear tall and regal, but his childish temper would make him less than an ideal lover. As no-nonsense as Lady Aldred seemed, the union might be ill-fated from the start.

Gavin walked through the hall in new clothes. He'd found them on his bed. A servant credited Lady Aldred with their appearance, as well as another change of clothes placed in the trunk at the foot of his bed. The woman thought of everything. He smoothed the wool tunic, glad again to be wearing something that fit his height.

In every way, he sensed he was now home. His youth had been spent here. It was at Kentwood he'd celebrated May Days and Christmases, learned to fight, to read and write, and where he'd first made love to a woman. He still remembered her advice to this day. She'd been twice his age, and with age came a supposed wisdom. She revealed he should never give his heart to a woman. Pleasure her. But never fall for her, for once a woman knew she held his heart, she would use that power to do him harm.

So he did as this long-ago, one-time lover instructed, though never really by intent. His heart simply remained intact over dozens of couplings, with women of all classes. He enjoyed the company of women. He enjoyed the act of lovemaking.

Yet no one stirred him until he'd held Lady Aldred's hand and planted a single kiss upon it. Not a one. And here she was, wife to his liege lord. The situation could not be any worse.

Unless he acted upon his desires.

He wouldn't. He couldn't. Gavin decided he must avoid contact with her. Move into the barracks with the majority of Aldred's guard, especially since he would be serving as their captain. No more eating at the head table. He would pretend to himself that Lady Aldred carried the Great Pestilence, and even a glance at her would cause him to keel over. His loyalty to Lord Aldred could not be suspect in any way. He'd always chosen to be an honorable man. It had not always been the way of his father, but he'd patterned himself more after Lord Aldred than Berwyn, at any rate.

Funny, how he thought of the man as Berwyn now. Of course, Gavin had been denounced by Berwyn. It made him wonder who his sire might truly be. With his mother gone, he doubted he would ever learn the identity of the man whose blood ran through him.

Rufus approached him. "I hear you will soon be captain of the guard at Kentwood, Gavin."

He shook his old friend's hand. "Only if the rumors I hear are true, Rufus. That you want to go to the wars in France?"

"Yes. I've wanted to for some time. Lord Aldred did not want to spare me, though, feeling I was too valuable here. Now 'tis my turn. Crecy is far in my past. I long for those days again."

A pretty wench passed in front of the men, catching Rufus's eye. "Excuse me, my lord," Rufus said, "but until I go, I'd better make the best use of my time." He followed the girl and pinched her bottom playfully.

Gavin laughed. He saw Robert pass Rufus, a smile on his face as he watched Rufus in hot pursuit of his conquest. Robert joined him. "I see Rufus never changes."

"Some men never do," Gavin agreed. "I must tell you, Robert, 'tis good spirits I am in tonight. I shall soon be captain of Lord Aldred's guard. Once I am in better shape, that is. 'Twas decided this very morn."

Robert smiled and slapped him on the back. "Then we have much to drink to, my friend. Being so close, 'twill be like the old days."

"Only no dying going on about us, eh?" Gavin studied his friend. "I take it that you have no plans to return to France?"

Robert shook his head sadly. "Father is much too ill now. The king has granted his request for me to remain behind. We have sent a good two score of men, though. Fondren is doing its part for England. And you, Gavin? I thought for sure you would miss the taste of battle. I am curious. Why settle here at Kentwood? Are you tired of those harsh, northern winters? Or should my curiosity be piqued for another reason?"

"I am sorry to hear of your father's poor health, Robert. And no, I have no plans to return to the war. I still have much to tell you."

"You've alluded to that. I—"

Their conversation was cut short by cheers. He glanced up to see Lord and Lady Aldred making their way down the stairs. Lord Aldred had his mahogany walking stick in hand, leaning on it heavily for support. His color looked better than it had this morning when they had spoken.

"Shall we greet them?" he asked Robert, and they made their way across the room.

"A good eve to all," Lord Aldred said as they approached. "I am glad you could come back and hear this troubadour, Robert. Elizabeth tells me I shall feel like a god once he has sung his ballads about me."

"Mayhap not a god, Husband," his wife teased.

"The Olympians are choosy about who graces their banquet table. More like Prometheus, I should think."

"I would say Heracles, my lord," added Gavin. "Half-mortal and half-god. Surely, you are on equal footing with such a legend?"

"Let us sit before you drive me mad with your prattle," the nobleman proclaimed.

"Come, Robert. Share my trencher with me tonight. I fear I dominated last night's conversation with Gavin. Besides," and he stole a swift look at his wife, "Elizabeth eats most of the food. I find there is nary a spare bite upon my trencher when she is by my side." The old warrior's eyes twinkled as much as his smile did.

Robert helped his host to his seat. Gavin escorted Lady Aldred. An awkward silence came between them. He sipped the wine set before him, not sure what to say. Finally, he broke the uncomfortable quiet.

"So, my lady, what have the harvests been like at Kentwood these last few years?"

With that simple question, she visibly relaxed. She spoke knowledgeably about the property and went into great detail, no matter what question he posed. He found himself enjoying their conversation immensely because she painted such a vivid picture as she spoke of Kentwood and its residents. She injected a wit into her stories that often caused him to smile. Just being in the presence of a woman again, one that was graceful and intelligent and lovely to look upon, was sheer pleasure.

Until they both reached for the salt cellar. As their fingers grazed against one another, Gavin sensed the spark that leaped between them. He glanced quickly to her and saw confusion in her eyes even as his loins stirred.

No! He could have no romantic attachment to the lady. There was Lord Aldred to consider. Even Robert, whom he knew had feelings for her. Gavin bent and fed a few scraps to Homer, who hovered at his feet, hoping to regain his composure in the process.

Yet as he rose again, how could he ignore what he saw? The full, pouting lips that ached to be kissed. The smooth, porcelain skin crying out for his touch. The burnished auburn curls he longed to rake his fingers through.

In prison, he rarely thought of a woman. That part of him seemed dead at the time. Survival was paramount. All he cared about was finding enough edible food or sleeping without a rat's bite awakening him. Luxuries to dream of consisted of warmth—the thick wool of a blanket or the rays of a summer sun beating down upon his back.

Yet his instant longing for this woman surpassed any urge he'd experienced in prison, more powerful than any others combined.

And she was the one untouchable thing in his life.

"I see the troubadour signaling me. He must be ready to begin tonight's performance." She rose from her seat. "If you will excuse me, Sir Gavin, I must see that things are put to rest."

She rushed off in a whirl of skirts. He watched her receding figure with an ache in his throat.

———

"Humor an old man, Gavin. Dance with Elizabeth," Aldred urged. "She loves to dance. I can't keep up with her anymore, especially with my dependence upon this walking stick. Besides, I am longing for my bed. My bones are creaking more loudly than usual."

Gavin watched a flush creep into Lady Aldred's cheeks. Or was it simply the shadows of the fire that played upon her satin skin?

Aldred tenderly kissed his wife's forehead. "Thank you for bringing the troubadour, my dear. He even got most of his facts correct."

She took her husband's hand. "No exaggeration, my lord?"

"None whatsoever. Ask Gavin or Robert. They were with me at some of those victories."

"Of course, I was but a small boy for the most part, my lord," Gavin said, an impish smile playing about his lips. "Mayhap the musician did overstate some of your abilities?"

"Nay, my boy. If anything, he did not quite do me justice enough. He missed some of my most memorable campaigns, in fact." Lord Aldred laughed and then waved a hand dismissively. "Now the music has started. I retire. Gavin, see that Elizabeth has a good time. I will hold you to it."

Gavin scooped Homer from his lap and placed him on the ground before he held his hand out to her. She hesitated a moment and then placed hers in his. A rotundellus was beginning, and so they joined the round circle of dancers. Elizabeth felt her steps became light, as light as her head felt. A giddiness consumed her, something she didn't understand.

They danced another rotundellus before a ductia started. She and Sir Gavin parted from the circle and then danced as a couple. She decided to ignore the dizziness that continued to sweep through her and simply enjoy the dancing. Sir Gavin proved to be a splendid partner, never treading upon her toes, holding her lightly yet firmly.

Robert interrupted and asked for a dance.

"I'm tired of watching you have all the fun, Gavin." He winked at her, and she curtseyed before the music began again.

Yet the entire time of their dance, she found her eyes searching for Sir Gavin. She was anxious to resume their partnership and secretly pleased when he reclaimed her for the next dance.

What's come over me?

As they danced, her pulse raced fast and her face felt flush, as if she'd drunk far too much wine. A warm tingle trickled through her as their new captain of the guard gazed into her eyes.

This is wrong. She knew it to be so but was powerless to act against it. She was more alive than she'd ever been.

"My lady." A tap on her shoulder stopped her in her tracks.

Nelia stood next to them. "'Tis Agnes. You must come now."

Elizabeth saw her bag in the servant's hands. It contained all she would need to help assist another babe into the world. She steeled herself for the task at hand. She had proven most competent at assisting women in childbirth over the years. She would never grow used to it, though.

"What ails this Agnes?" asked Sir Gavin.

She shook off the gloom that had enveloped her. "'Tis nothing, my lord. Simply a woman ready to give birth." She took the sack from Nelia and held it up to him and smiled. "My tools of the trade."

"I shall accompany you. 'Tis far you must go? Are you in need of a horse?"

"No, my lord. Agnes's hut is but a half-mile from here. I can easily—"

"'Tis late. Lord Aldred would not have you go alone."

She saw in his face that he would have no argument from her.

"Very well, then."

They left the castle, going down the long steps, through the inner and outer baileys, and arriving at the gates. Sir Gavin turned and chuckled. She watched as he picked up the kitten which had followed them and murmured something in its ear before setting it down. The furball scampered away as if headed back to the great hall. The knight then signaled for the gates to be opened.

"Be watchful for when we return," he ordered the gatekeeper.

She noted the authority in his voice. He was used to commanding men—and being obeyed. Despite her earlier, girlish longings toward him, she bristled at his tone. In a blink of an eye, he sounded like her father and most noblemen of her acquaintance. She had learned to treasure her relationship with Aldred. He had proven the exception among men. Elizabeth would cower under no man, not even one she was drawn to.

They walked the distance in silence. She mulled over what must be done, and her escort seemed to sense she needed the quiet to prepare.

When they arrived at the cottage, she told him, "You may return to the castle, my lord. 'Tis a long night ahead of me. I doubt 'twill end before dawn since first babes take their sweet time before they make their appearance in the world. It will be safe to return in the morning light."

He did not budge. "And I shall wait for you here, my lady. You are under my protection." He crossed his arms over his chest.

"Very well."

She did not want to argue. He would be out of her sight, as no men were ever allowed to witness births. If they were, then she assumed far less births would occur.

She knocked and received no reply to enter. Her brow furrowed as she entered the humble hut. A fire burned low in the hearth. That would be the first item on her list. She scanned the room and saw no one there.

"How odd," she mused.

"My lady?"

Elizabeth spotted Agnes on a pallet at the far side of the room. "No one is here," she whispered when she sensed Sir Gavin behind her. She looked over her shoulder and said, "Usually several women gather for a delivery of a babe."

His brow wrinkled in thought. "Might they still be at Kentwood? The dancing was in full swing as we left."

She cursed under her breath. "Nelia no doubt told no others. That silly servant grows senile on me."

"Will that be a problem? Have you not aided in childbirth before?"

Annoyance flashed through her. "Of course I have," she hissed. "I am used to having women follow my orders, 'tis all. 'Twill now take longer for me to accomplish what must be done, with no other hands to support me."

"Then I shall help."

She laughed. "You? A man aid in birthing a child? That won't do at all."

Just then Agnes moaned. Elizabeth rushed to the woman's side and bent close.

"'Tis Lady Elizabeth, Agnes. I've come to help you with your babe."

Agnes began to weep. "Oh, thank you, my lady, thank you. I must have this child. I must."

She brushed back the girl's hair from her face. "Of course, dear. I know Peter would be proud." She stood. "Just let me get organized."

She returned to Sir Gavin. "The fire must be built up and water put on to boil. Can you manage that?"

He grunted. "I have built a fire or two in my time, my lady. Boiling the water may prove to be difficult, though." He grinned and walked outside to where the wood supply lay and brought in several logs, placing them on the fire.

Elizabeth ignored him and busied herself with her preparations. As hot water became available, she washed her hands carefully. She explained in hushed tones to Sir Gavin, "Agnes lost her husband Peter last month. He worked in the stables and was kicked in the head by a hot-blooded horse. He lived a few days before passing on. 'Tis why this first and only babe is so important to her."

He nodded. "A link between her and her dead spouse. I understand."

She watched as he went to Agnes and bent, taking her hand. "We will see this babe born, Agnes. You have no need to worry. You are not alone. Everything will work out. God will watch over us this night."

Elizabeth watched as the weeping girl squeezed his hand, approving of his comforting tone. She realized Sir Gavin couldn't imagine being in Agnes's position. No husband. Alone in the world. Ready to give birth. Still, he offered a stranger solace all the same.

She took a deep breath and prayed that this birth would go well as she focused on delivering the babe.

───────

Lady Aldred worked him like a commander worked his soldiers on a battlefield, only she was far more driven.

"Open the door again," she said as she twisted the lid of a jar free and rubbed salve over Agnes's belly. "And if you spy a rope with a knot in it, undo it. Opening things up 'twill ease your pain, Agnes," she told the frightened young woman.

Gavin did as asked. Lady Aldred issued commands one after the other. He could see why she had been uneasy to find no assistance available. He had no idea birth was such a complicated affair. Throughout it all, she took time, though, to comfort Agnes.

"You are doing a remarkable job, Agnes. What a good girl you are. Your babe will be so lucky to have such a wonderful mother as you," she praised.

Still, despite the noblewoman's reassuring words, Agnes's screams rose again and again. Sweat broke out on Gavin's brow as he watched her writhe and moan between contractions. The pain the girl endured was remarkable. Both her bravery and that of Lady Aldred's surpassed anything he ever saw on the battlefield. How Lady Aldred kept from falling apart continually surprised him. He found himself growing weak from simply watching such an ordeal.

Finally, the babe came. She signaled him to move closer. He saw the crown of a head appear.

"Help catch it," she whispered as she steadied Agnes's legs, holding them firmly. "That's right,

Agnes. Now push. One more time, a really hard push. That's what we need. The head is coming through, Agnes, but your babe needs you to do this one last thing. One more strong push, my girl, and 'twill all be over."

Agnes did as told. If Gavin thought her screams were loud before, he thought she might die with the last one. More animal than human, it was a keening wail that came through dry, cracked lips.

And then the babe squirted from her body. He brought his hands around it, afraid he would drop it. What if he hurt something so tiny?

"'Tis a boy, Agnes," Lady Aldred proclaimed. "A healthy boy. You can hear from his lusty cry how glad he is to have finally arrived."

Gavin's nerves nearly shattered as the babe slithered and slipped in his large hands.

"I must cut the cord then tend to Agnes," Lady Aldred said quietly to him. "There is much bleeding, more than usual. You must care for the babe."

"Me?" He was dumbfounded. "'Tis the first babe I've ever held."

"Well, make yourself useful, my lord. I've set out all that you need. The babe must be washed and then rubbed down with salt. See to it. And be gentle about it."

She returned to her patient and cut the cord that bound mother to her babe. Once free, Gavin did as he was told. The baby boy quieted as he worked. Large, dark eyes stared up at him in wonder. Gavin thrilled to have such a miracle of life within his grasp. He understood in an instant how much it would pain a mother to send her son off to war, knowing he could be lost in the blink of an eye during battle.

This babe had the rest of his life ahead of him.

Gavin bonded with the child, knowing that he, too, had begun a new life after escaping from prison.

"Now, rinse the salt from him. Cleanse his mouth with honey," Lady Aldred instructed over her shoulder. "There's some in the pot next to you. Can you swaddle him?"

"Can I... what 'tis this swaddling?"

"Never mind. I'm almost through here."

She finished her tasks and wrapped a blanket around Agnes. She came and took the clean babe from Gavin's arms and swaddled the child tightly, her moves efficient and practiced.

Smiling down, she asked the infant, "Are you ready to nurse, little love? Your mama wants to see you."

She brought the babe over to Agnes. Both women cooed over him. Lady Aldred began to teach Agnes and her babe how to nurse. Gavin, embarrassed, walked out the cottage door and drew a deep breath. Dawn had broken. A new day. One where he could say he had helped bring a new life into this world.

An immense sense of pride filled him. Of all he had ever accomplished, this night and his small part in birthing the little boy meant the most.

He heard chattering voices and saw two women come from around the side of the cottage.

They curtseyed and eyed him curiously. "We've come to check on Agnes, my lord. We do every morning for the past week. Her babe will come any day now," one informed him.

"Then you can say hello to her and her new son," he replied. "She gave birth minutes ago to a hale and hearty lad."

Both women squealed in delight and rushed into the hut. Lady Aldred emerged a few minutes later, her clothes and hair disheveled, a happy glow across her cheeks.

"They will take care of the rest. We are free to return to the castle."

He took the bag from her as they began to walk back. "You are a hard worker, my lady. Do you do this very often?"

She shrugged. "A few times a month. More often close to Michaelmas. I suppose more babes are begun in the cold winter months." She smiled shyly at him.

"You seem in good spirits."

"I am," she agreed. "You think I would be worn to the bone after no sleep and such a long ordeal. Yet for a few minutes after, I am exhilarated, happy for the mother and her child."

"Have you ever longed for your own babe?"

He could have kicked himself for asking, simply from the shadow that crossed her face.

"I suppose 'tis not meant to be," she replied quietly. "I do not mind. I have never really wanted any of my own. I have Lord Aldred to care for. And Kentwood."

"But every woman wants a babe in her arms. 'Tis a beautiful expression of a couple's love," he reasoned.

"I'm not every woman," she snapped. "I don't need love. Children, I mean. I have all I want in Kentwood and my husband. A woman's worth should not be judged by her ability to produce a child."

She lifted her skirts and raced off. Gavin quickly caught up with her. He grabbed her elbow and whirled her around.

"I must apologize, my lady," he began.

"You have no need to be sorry. I... I..." Her voice trailed off, and she began to cry, great gasping sobs.

He didn't know if it was because she was tired or for his insensitive remarks, but he knew he was responsible for her tears. He'd never been able to watch a woman cry, especially not as hard as Lady Aldred now did. That he'd caused her this pain upset him more than he cared to admit.

He dropped the bag and enfolded her in his arms. "There now. Hush. 'Twill be all right." He held her close, one hand running through her silken locks. "Shush. You will be fine."

She raised a tear-stained face to his, her mouth trembling. With no thought to the consequences, Gavin bent his head and touched his lips to hers.

14

Fear struck Elizabeth just as Sir Gavin's lips met hers. *A kiss! What was he thinking?* She could not kiss him. She didn't kiss anyone. Aldred's feeble attempts over the years flittered into her mind. She stiffened in his arms.

Her hesitation did not stop him, though. His lips slowly brushed against hers. She realized the sensation was most pleasant. It caused a ripple of heat to run through her. His hand stroked her hair. Her scalp tingled. Her body relaxed.

Panic set in suddenly. She tensed again. She didn't know what to do, how to respond. Yet respond she did, as if her body were no longer her own. Her knees grew watery. She gripped his shoulders for support. He pulled her closer still. His arms wrapped firmly around her, drawing her into a muscled chest.

And still his lips worked their magic, now nipping her lower one, teasing her. He licked the corner of her mouth and then trailed kisses along her jaw. Her head fell back. A shudder rushed up her spine.

This is Heaven.

His kisses continued along her exposed throat.

She began to throb everywhere. Her fingers kneaded his shoulders as his cat's paws might. She heard a noise that sounded like a satisfied growl come from him.

Then his lips were gone. A shiver passed through her as the gentle breeze blew. She opened her eyes, only to meet him gazing down at her. He brushed a kiss against her temple, another one on her cheek. The slow play of his mouth began again as he caressed her. The throbbing built within her, starting an ache that clamored for a something she hadn't a clue how to satisfy.

Elizabeth opened her mouth to speak, to ask what was happening. Sir Gavin's fingers, tangled in her curls, caught them and pulled slightly, forcing her head back. His eyes glowed. The yellow rings blended into the warm brown, a heat in them that frightened and excited her at the same time.

Then his mouth was upon hers, gentle no longer. She clung to him. His tongue demanded to mate with hers, taking, taking. Again and again he took from her, even her very breath, until she no longer knew where she ended and he began. His arms pinned her against him. Her breasts ached. Her bones melted. A dizziness swept across her. She wanted this to go on. Forever.

A rooster crowed in the distance. It brought her to her senses. She broke their embrace.

"I cannot do this," she gasped. "I cannot. I am married. Aldred." Her voice trailed off, as no further words would come. She stiffened her spine and locked her knees to keep from collapsing back into the knight's arms, back into their inviting warmth.

Every pore screamed that she had betrayed her husband. A deep shame filled her as she looked at Sir

Gavin. He stood before her, his breathing harsh and ragged, his eyes full of smoldering desire.

The shame was compounded by guilt, because despite her disloyalty to Aldred, Elizabeth wanted this man more than anything she'd ever wanted, even more than Kentwood. The thought brought an icy fear. Nothing had ever been more important than her home and the power she wielded here. And now one kiss, from a man she didn't particularly like, threatened her very existence.

She raised her chin haughtily and pictured ice running through her veins. These feelings must end, here and now. She would think of it as a particularly difficult judgment, when it hurt her to rule in one party's favor, against another. No sentimentality, no weakness, could be displayed.

"I do not welcome such attentions, my lord. You are never to touch me again."

She saw hurt spring to his eyes. Quickly, it was replaced by a steely resolve.

"My apologies, my lady," he said stiffly. He turned and picked up the bag he'd dropped during their embrace and began walking stoically toward the castle.

Elizabeth fell into step beside him, though not too closely. They remained in silence until they reached the gates. Sir Gavin signaled for their opening.

She turned to him, longing to reach out and touch his stubbled cheek. While he stood tall and straight as the soldier he was, her thoughts whirled incoherently.

"I bid you goodnight. Or I suppose, a good morn."

Handing her bag to her, he bowed formally and strode across the yard in the opposite direction of the keep.

She watched him go with a regret that weighed

heavily on her. She bit her lip to keep from crying out to him.

And what would she say if she did speak? Would she beg him to come back and hold her as if she were the dearest thing to him on earth? To ask him to run his hot lips along her throat? To promise her that he would never let go, no matter what fate tossed their way?

She shook her head, tamping down the bitter laughter that threatened to escape her lips. Blindly she made her way to the solar, seeing nothing before her but his image, still feeling his hands push through her hair and his heated mouth upon hers.

She pushed open the door of the solar. Wearily, she stripped down to her chemise and drew the curtain back from her side of the bed. As she slipped in, Aldred's even breathing was the only sound in the room. Usually, it comforted her.

But it didn't now. And she didn't know if it ever would. Not after those magical, stolen moments with a handsome knight at dawn.

She turned and pulled the curtain again. Rising panic flooded through her. Would her thumping heart awaken Aldred from his deep sleep?

How could she explain anything to him? With one look, all the trust he had in her would flee. Her husband had given her everything, met her every whim, saw to her every desire.

Except one...

Who knew what she really desired? She hadn't known. Not until Sir Gavin's kiss awakened a sleeping dragon within her. A greedy dragon who wanted more. Much more.

Silently, she cursed him. What had he done to her?

And worse. What would she now do?

———

He thought the hellhole in France his worst nightmare. That memory seemed like child's play compared to what he now endured.

Gavin craved a woman, more than he'd ever thought possible, with a fierce longing that brought a physical ache deep inside, as if a sharp sword had been run through him.

And Lady Aldred was the one woman he could never have. How could he betray Lord Aldred in such a manner? The old nobleman had been more than a father to him. He now saved Gavin from a living nightmare. How could he covet his lord's lady?

Much less serve Aldred, defend him and his property. Even defend the very wife Gavin so desired.

What solution could he seek?

His first thought was to leave immediately. Go to Robert. If he asked to serve Robert's father, he would have little contact with either Aldred or his young wife. More than likely, being new, he would be among the soldiers contracted to the king. His return to the wars in France would be a strong probability.

The thought made his heart heavy. He'd lost so much already. Coming back to Kentwood, after the crushing blow he'd suffered during the short time he'd seen Berwyn, seemed like coming to his true home. Disappointment ruled his life.

He straightened his shoulders. He refused to turn bitter. He was grateful to be alive after all he'd endured in France. He decided to head toward the barracks. He was ready to begin training again. He *needed* to train again, needed the sheer physicality of swinging a sword with but a single purpose in mind.

And Gavin needed to find in his heart what he would say to Aldred.

15

Elizabeth opened her eyes. Sleep had finally come, despite her earlier restlessness. She had tried to will her limbs to stay still. Disturbing Aldred was unthinkable, especially since he often slept fitfully.

"A problem, my dear?"

She turned her head and saw that the bed curtains were pulled back. Her husband sat in a chair across from the bed, his walking stick in hand. He offered her a gentle smile, which made her feel traitorous. She couldn't admit to kissing Sir Gavin at any price.

Or could she?

Should she place the blame on the handsome knight? Insist that he leave? He and Robert were close. She knew Robert would take in his friend, especially if Sir Gavin shared with him his terrible plight.

No, thinking like that was selfish and dishonorable. She'd been neither in years. She had grown from a self-centered brat to a woman of destiny, thanks to the confidence and support of her husband. She would manage the predicament.

"No, nothing is wrong, my lord. I'm just a bit

tired, I suppose. Agnes delivered her babe early this morning, a fine, healthy boy. 'Twas long and difficult, and especially hard, I would think, with Peter now gone."

"Does she need anything?"

The concern on Aldred's face showed what a kind, caring liege she'd married. She admired his still-noble bearing, his warrior spirit, and his gentle ways.

"I believe things can be arranged to satisfy everyone concerned. Of course," she said, as she swung her legs from the bed and sat up, "it might include a bit of matchmaking."

"You? Meddle?" He laughed heartily. "I never would dream of my lovely wife intervening in affairs of the heart."

A mischievous smile pulled at the corners of her mouth. "I know. It doesn't sound much like me, does it?"

They both laughed before he asked, "Whom have you selected for our Agnes?"

She paused. "I'll admit a candidate springs to mind. I'll see to it today. 'Tis one of your guard, Aldred. A young soldier, just a year older than Agnes herself. Might we spare him? Move him to the stables?"

Aldred thought on it. "Regardless of who this young man is, I doubt he'll want to move. 'Tis hard for a soldier to settle in to domestic life, but do as you wish. Make him an offer."

He paused a minute and then added, "You might wish to speak to Gavin about it, though."

Simply hearing Sir Gavin's name caused Elizabeth's cheeks to burn. "Why?" she asked, a bit too sharply.

"Why, you ask? Well, he is now captain of the

guard, Wife. I would think he would make the final decision concerning one of his men."

"They are your men, Aldred," she asserted. "I hardly think—"

"I insist," he said. "He should be informed. Besides, Gavin needs to see the formidable enemy he's up against."

Her husband's words puzzled her. "Who?"

Aldred chuckled. "Why, you, my love."

She protested, her voice rising in hysteria. "I am not the enemy. By what—"

"Calm yourself," he ordered. "You usually don't ruffle so easily when teased." He studied her.

Her guilt over the kiss burned within her. She should confess. Now. Let him punish her as he may.

Yet no admission left her lips as Aldred stood and moved closer to her. Placing a hand against her cheek, he asked, "Do you feel well?"

She cradled his hand in her own. "Never better, my lord."

"Then go speak to Gavin when you are dressed. Put on that pretty green cotehardie that matches your eyes. I so love to see you in it."

He kissed her cheek. "I'm going for a bit of a turn." He moved toward the door. "I shall see you later."

Elizabeth watched him go. Her first thoughts had been to wear one of her favorite cotehardies. Not that she sought to appear attractive to Sir Gavin, of course. She simply wanted to wear something luxurious. She needed to feel her full power as she faced him, to feel in control.

And not feel as if she would throw herself into his arms at first sight.

She called for water in which to bathe. If she took a little extra care this morning, who would notice?

Certainly not Sir Gavin. Elizabeth was sure after their acrimonious parting that he would not think too kindly of her.

Still, she would look and feel the authority she held. She prepared herself inside and out, much as a soldier going into battle would. She guessed it would be a battle of wits and wills between her and their new captain.

She was certain she would prevail.

As she entered the great hall a few minutes later, she spied Nelia and signaled her over.

"Please send for Sir Gavin. I am not sure where he can be found, but be quick about it."

"Why, Sir Gavin is in the training yard."

"What?"

Nelia nodded. "As of today, it looks as if he is demonstrating his fine form."

Two passing servants giggled and fluttered their eyelashes at Nelia's words. One dropped a pitcher she was carrying. The loud crash of pottery upon the floor drew every eye in the hall and caused Sir Gavin's hovering cat to flee the room.

Nelia latched onto the offender's shoulder. "Enough of that. Clean up this mess at once." Elizabeth watched the look Nelia gave as she took in both girls. "And no more excuses to head to the bailey again, either of you."

The servant turned back to her mistress. "I'll fetch Sir Gavin myself, my lady."

Elizabeth's curiosity piqued. "No, I will speak with him later." She quickly rolled off her orders for the day, knowing that Nelia would see to everything. Almost against her will, she decided to head to the outer bailey, where the soldiers usually went through their training exercises.

The noise of clanging swords sounded long before she reached the open area. The ringing was rapid, hard, brutal. As she turned the corner, she saw a crowd gathered around the training area. The looks on the faces she saw told her the story. Some were enraptured. Some smiled. Others showed sheer amazement on their faces.

Elizabeth pushed through the throng until she arrived at the front. She spied Sir Gavin fighting two soldiers at once. Sheer determination adorned his features as he called instructions. She didn't often watch the guards drill, but even she knew an amazing display of skill when she saw it.

Sir Gavin called for a third man to enter the fray against him. Her heart caught in her throat. She knew no harm should come to him, seeing as how it was merely an exercise. That, coupled with his great skill, assured her he would be fine. She calmed her nerves and studied the scene before her.

He was thinner than a man his height should be, but that didn't surprise her, considering his ordeal in France. Still, he had escaped a few months earlier, and she was sure he'd put on some weight. Muscle, too, as she remembered his hardened chest from their kiss.

His arms were bare. Sinewy muscles in his forearms gleamed with sweat as he danced from one opponent to the next. Sweat also caused his tunic to cling to him, outlining the stretched muscles across his back.

What must he have been in his prime, before languishing two years in a forgotten prison cell? The man before her would be envied by many men, and sought after by even more women. A primal beauty was evident in his swordplay. It was like a song, only physical. His sword flowed with a strength and power so graceful that it took her breath away, much as the man himself did. Sir Gavin would be a formidable foe on the battlefield.

"Halt!" The word echoed throughout the bailey. He brushed the sweat from his brow with his forearm. "We will break for now. 'Tis close to the noon meal. We will resume training afterward. Wash up and head to the great hall."

As the soldiers and the crowd gathered about begin to disperse, his gaze locked with hers. He began to make his way to her. Displeasure radiated from his body.

As he drew near, Elizabeth said, "We need to talk."

Their new captain gave her an odd look, and she realized he had spoken the same words at the same time. It caused her to flush, the burn riding from her neck and spilling onto her cheeks. This wasn't how she wanted their conversation to be. She wanted to speak calmly, rationally, with the man. Why did a single look from him unnerve her so?

He waved a hand to his left, and they moved away from the others, rounding a corner. A water trough stood there. He leaned over and plunged his head straight into it, then pulled it back out, beads of water clinging to his skin in the sunlight. He slicked back his raven hair and bent again, splashing water upon his face several times.

"Forgive me for addressing you in such a state, my lady. I had no idea you would be present and wish to speak to me."

She looked at him coolly, but all she really knew was she now gazed upon the most magnificent specimen she'd ever looked upon. Many suitors came to her door before her marriage to Aldred, some of them quite handsome and charming. Of course, she'd never given any of them a second thought, even those who gazed at her with sweet longing.

This man was different. The way he held himself, his head high, his eyes level. Elizabeth was aware of the rippling power flowing through him, the sharp planes of his face, the lips now curled in a slight sneer.

Oh, Mary, Mother of God, how she longed to touch those lips, stroke his cheek, be enveloped in his arms again!

Instead, she tamped down her emotions and spoke evenly.

"That's quite all right, my lord. I have but a simple matter to discuss with you."

She almost began to fidget as she had in her younger days, but she willed her hands to stay by her side. No wiggling, no nail biting. She would give him no sign of the discomfort she experienced in his presence.

If only he would back away from her, their conversation might be easier to begin. He stood close. Not so close as to seem improper, but too close for her comfort. He was male, all male, and his very scent threatened to overpower her and cause her to swoon.

He frowned. "I don't see that we have anything to discuss, my lady."

"Then, why did you wish to speak with me?" she threw back at him. He remained silent, seeming to bite back words he longed to say.

"I am here to address you on the matter of Agnes," she finally said.

His expression softened in an instant. "Is she well? Is the babe all right? What might I do?"

Without thinking, Gavin had cupped Lady Aldred's elbow. He almost cursed aloud at the spark that flashed between them. He quickly dropped his hand to his side. She stood there, her soft lips parted slightly, her head tilted as she looked at him.

The woman was breathtaking. Her rich cote-hardie of green, the color of forest moss, reflected the very shade of her eyes. That thick, abundant hair spilled about her shoulders in glorious waves, a simple gold circlet taming the auburn waves.

He hungered to possess her sweet mouth and make it his again, for her curves to be pressed to him. Desire flooded him as never before. He dropped his gaze to the ground. He needed the simple action to gain his composure.

As he stared downward, she said, "No, the two are fine. What I'm looking for is a husband."

His head shot up. He saw her blush furiously. Her words were calm, though.

"I need a husband for Agnes. 'Tis a sweet girl she is, and she and the babe need someone to provide for them."

She turned away from him, her hands behind her back. She began pacing as a general who discussed his plans for battle with his officers. She spit out her words succinctly, expecting no questions.

"I have decided upon one of my husband's soldiers as her mate. He is a young man, no more than eight-and-ten. He's a shy one, and I do not think him totally suited for a military life. I would make him an offer to replace Peter in the stables and marry Agnes. Naturally, he would accept the babe as his own and raise it with love and a firm hand."

"Naturally," Gavin echoed. He found himself amused by her plan for others, wondering if anyone ever told her no.

"If you are agreeable—and I consult you only because Lord Aldred insisted I must—I will approach
young Emery today. He can move from the barracks
to the stables tonight. They can be wed as soon as
Agnes is churched and up and about."

He decided to challenge her. "And if I'll not agree
to this plan, whom would you have her wed after
young Emery?"

Elizabeth turned. Her mouth dropped in surprise.
She snapped it shut, her eyes narrowing. "I see no
reason why this cannot be. I am certain you'll agree.
Emery, too."

"If I don't? Will you tattle to Lord Aldred?"

She bristled visibly, her voice rising. "I will not
tattle on anyone, my lord, and if I should, 'twould be
you I tattled about!" She gave a very unladylike snort
and tapped her foot impatiently.

"And yourself, my lady," he prodded gently. "I do
believe you were party to the tattling offense." He saw
her temper truly flare. He allowed her to see his smile
now, the one he'd tried hard to keep hidden while he
baited her.

"Why, you act as a mischievous boy!" she proclaimed. A look of joy crossed her face. The air was
knocked from him at the radiant smile she bestowed
upon him. "No one teases me at all, except my husband, of course. And sometimes Robert, though I fear
he'll never quite get the hang of it."

"No one else, my lady?"

She frowned. "No. None. I fear some might think
me quite unapproachable. I make a good deal of the
decisions that concern Kentwood, as well as render
many of the judgments when a protest occurs, be it
over a disputed bit of garden or squabbling over the
ownership of a pig. No one challenges my word." A

thoughtful look crossed her face. "Not even Aldred nowadays," she said wistfully.

"I assure you, my lady, that you may have young Emery for your stable and your Agnes. In the short time I have observed him, I have seen he does not have the makings of a good soldier and would be better suited for other tasks. I shall not protest his loss."

Lady Aldred beamed. "I shall guarantee Emery will accept my offer. Agnes is a pretty thing, with a sweet disposition. She will make a good wife to him. 'Twill also prevent him from going to France, as Kentwood soon owes the king another twenty men."

"Then I shall bid you good day," Gavin said with false cheer.

He wanted nothing more than to keep her here, chatting away so relaxed and animated, but he could think of nothing else to say. He knew, too, that it would be dangerous to remain alone here with her, the others having made their way to the keep. For once, he did not trust himself—and what he might do. Lady Aldred proved far too tempting and he needed her gone.

"My lady! My lady! Come quick!"

Gavin looked over as Nelia rounded the corner, her skirts hiked high as she ran toward them.

"'Tis Lord Aldred. He's fallen. You must come at once!"

16

Aldred moaned as someone lifted him from the floor. Bolts of lightning sizzled through his head and caused great flashes of light. Darkness followed the flashes, accompanied by roars not unlike waves crashing upon rock. Dull throbs pounded in his skull. They trickled down to his chest.

He longed to open his eyes. It would require too much effort. He left them closed. Jostling meant they took him up the stairs, to his solar.

Elizabeth... His mind cried out to his wife, the rock upon which he had built these twilight years. He had had affection for all his wives, and his children, too—but Elizabeth had become most precious of all. He had watched her grow from a pampered child to a woman of efficiency and deep maturity. He taught her to hone her keen intelligence and trust in her good judgment. As she had matured, she had even gained compassion.

And a radiant beauty. He'd not seen a woman her equal in all his years, not in France nor in the whole of England. It would be fitting that, with his death, the child of his heart would now marry the child from his loins, the son he had never known was his until these last few end of days.

They would be a perfect match. They would keep Kentwood true to course. He imagined their children playing hide and seek throughout the castle and chuckled to himself. The sound came out as a weak groan.

Voices fluttered about him. Hands touched him. They placed him upon his bed. The familiar smells of his solar settled about him, giving him comfort.

He frowned and wished everyone would leave. He was dying. He knew it. He wished to do so in peace, not with half of Kentwood's people surrounding him. Elizabeth would understand that.

If only she would come...

———

Elizabeth tore up the steps at breakneck speed, her slippers clicking as she ran down the stone corridor to the solar. Sir Gavin and Nelia followed her. She could wait for no one. She must reach Aldred.

Out of breath, she paused and collected herself before entering the room. It would not do for him to see her so flustered. When she stepped inside, amazement followed.

The solar held close to twenty, no, thirty people. All gathered around the bed, speaking rapidly, fussing amongst themselves.

"What do you think you are doing?"

Her voice rang out, bringing those present to instant silence. She took a calming breath.

"I would ask that everyone leave," she said, politely but very firmly. "I know you are all concerned for Lord Aldred, but I will see to his injuries and then ask for any needed help."

A buzzing began, with each voice expressing a different opinion.

"Now," she said, her tone low and threatening, "is not the time to challenge my words, nor my instructions." She glared at those in front of her. Immediately, the crowd began to part.

As she moved toward the bed, she sensed the room vacating. She turned and saw only Sir Gavin and Nelia standing there. Both awaited her orders.

As the room emptied, she motioned to them.

"Come. And close the door."

Nelia did. They both hurried quickly to the bed. Elizabeth already studied Aldred as they approached. His brow furrowed as if in pain or deep concentration. He lay atop the bedclothes, his clothes slightly askew.

"Tell me what happened, Nelia."

Elizabeth leaned over and stroked her husband's brow. Immediately, his body visibly relaxed, so she continued the soothing motion. She also took his hand in hers. It felt cold to the touch.

"I looked up from my duties and saw Lord Aldred making his way down the stairs, a proud look upon his face. His walking stick was in his hand. He raised a hand in greeting to me," Nelia recalled. "Then, with but two steps remaining, an odd look appeared upon his face, as if something surprised him."

Nelia stopped, and Sir Gavin touched the old servant's shoulder. "Go on," he urged.

The woman patted his hand and continued. "He crumpled up and tumbled the short way down. I called for help and went looking for Lady Elizabeth."

"You did well," the knight assured her.

Elizabeth nodded and ran her hands along Aldred's limbs in a thorough inspection.

"No broken bones," she said, a sense of relief coming for a brief moment. She leaned close to his ear. "Can you hear me, Aldred? 'Tis Elizabeth, come to tend you. You gave me quite a scare."

A shadow of a smile crossed her husband's pale face. His eyelids fluttered a few times and opened for a moment before drifting closed again.

She took his face in both her hands and pressed a kiss to his brow. "Wake up, you sweet old goat," she said teasingly. "I would not have you play games anymore with me."

His eyes opened again and remained that way. He mumbled something.

"What's that?" She bent low, her ear close to his mouth. *"Courlieu?"* she repeated. "Did you say *courlieu*?"

She took his hand between hers and rubbed it, trying to warm it. "Yes, you sent the *courlieu* to the king but a few days ago, dearest. He has barely had time to reach London, much less return with a message for you. Don't worry about that now."

"No time..." Aldred's words were but a bare whisper.

Elizabeth looked at him. She saw the life begin to ebb from his eyes. She looked to Nelia.

"Get the priest," she mouthed, not wanting Aldred to hear her words. She turned back to her husband.

"Fight, Aldred. Stay with me." A tear coursed down her cheek.

Aldred looked at her. "So... sorry. Gavin?"

He stepped forward. "I am here, my lord." He

knelt opposite Elizabeth and took Aldred's free hand. "Please rest. Do not try and speak."

"Late. Gavin, my boy... Robert..." Aldred sighed. "My Elizabeth."

She pressed his knuckles to her mouth. "I'm here, Husband. I shall not leave you. You must promise the same." Her voice started to falter. "Stay with me. Do not leave me, Aldred. Please. I cannot bear you to go."

"Kentwood... safe... Edward... missive..."

Hot tears began to stream down her cheeks. "Kentwood is fine, my love. King Edward will not let anything happen to it. Rest, dearest. Rest."

She closed her eyes, willing her youth and strength to flow from her into Aldred. His grasp on her hand grew weaker, though. She knew his time had drawn nigh.

"Oh, Aldred," she whispered. "You have taught me so much. I do love you so."

He smiled. His eyes clouded over. "Be... with you... always."

"Yes," she encouraged him. "Always and forever."

A rustling caused her to turn around. Kentwood's priest had arrived. Elizabeth admitted to herself that death was but a moment away. She nodded to the priest, and he came to the bed.

"Do what you must," she said, "but I will not leave his side."

The cleric nodded and began the last rites. The Latin lulled her into a half-dream state. Moments from time flickered across as she recalled her wedding. Her wedding night. Aldred's patience as he taught her to read and write. Riding together. Sharing meals. Sitting side by side at mass. At feasts. Judgment days.

It had been a good life for them. Not a typical

marriage, but successful, nonetheless. Kentwood had flourished. Aldred could go to his death, proud that his land and people thrived.

Then the slight pressure on her hand ceased. The priest continued on in the ritual. Elizabeth looked over to Sir Gavin, who held Aldred's other hand. His eyes glittered with unshed tears. His mouth was tight. He looked ready to snap at any moment. But when he met her gaze, a sudden look of helplessness appeared in his eyes. His shoulders slumped in defeat. She wondered how many times he'd had to stand by on the battlefield and watch as a comrade died.

"I'm sorry," he whispered, his voice low.

She closed her eyes. With her husband's death, her true nightmare began. The day she dreaded had now finally arrived. Her destiny was no longer in her own hands.

17

Gavin entered the great hall for the evening meal. Training had occupied his body that day, but his thoughts never strayed far from Elizabeth and her welfare. Aldred had rested in the ground two weeks now. During that time, Gavin watched as Elizabeth drove herself harder and harder, day after day, as if by making Kentwood perfect, it would bring her husband back to life again.

His eyes scanned the crowded room, looking past servants moving trestle tables into place. He spied her, deep in conversation with Cedd. He moved toward them, Homer close on his heels, and caught Cedd's eye. The steward nodded imperceptibly to him. As he reached them, Cedd ended the conversation.

"Here is Sir Gavin, my lady," he told Elizabeth. "Surely estate business can wait, at least until you've filled your belly with a meal." Cedd looked at Elizabeth with disapproval. "You must slow down. You must eat."

"Yes," Elizabeth said. "I know. 'Tis that food seems to have lost its appeal for me." She sighed. "We will begin again after..."

"After you break your fast on the morrow," Gavin interrupted. He looked from one to the other. "'Twill be plenty of time to discuss what requires my lady's attention, will it not, Cedd?"

The steward nodded. "Yes, my lord." He bowed and left them alone.

Gavin smiled and held a hand out to her. "May I escort you to supper, my lady? I'm sure you will find plenty of food there that requires your attention."

"Of course." She placed her hand upon his sleeve, and they walked to the dais. Gavin seated her and then himself. He signaled for wine to be poured.

After their cups were filled, he held his up. "A toast, my lady. To all you have done and to the future prosperity of Kentwood."

She gave his words a sad smile. "To Kentwood." She took a deep pull on the wine and then set down her cup.

Servants appeared with their trencher, soon accompanied by starling, cold pork, and a few side dishes. He tore a piece from the pork and placed it under his seat. Homer immediately attacked his dinner. A large round of cheese arrived and was also placed before them.

He looked at the food and said, "Surely, some of this tempts you? Cedd is right. Even the hardworking mistress of Kentwood must take time from her busy day to eat."

She shrugged. "I have no appetite these days. I find so much to attend to. The spring planting must be finished and one field of vines is left to be pruned. And I am certain the king will soon request an additional number of men now that the weather has warmed. You know the nature of warfare, my lord. 'Twill begin again in earnest, now that milder weather has arrived. And the sheep need to be put out to pasture, too."

"I would hope you would not run yourself into an early grave, my lady. You must eat."

Elizabeth wrinkled her nose. "Food holds no attraction for me."

"You wish to shrink into nothing? Pray put a few bites in your mouth. Even a soldier on the march must keep up his strength."

Gavin leaned in closer to her. "Your people worry about you, my lady. They see you working non-stop from dawn until far into the night. You must rest. 'Tis not a race you are running."

She looked at him earnestly. "Oh, but 'tis just that very thing, my lord. I wrote the king of Aldred's death a fortnight ago. I believe I have at least time through inspecting the beehives in May and possibly the cutting and drying of the hay in June before he replies. If lucky, I may be able to supervise the wheat harvest in July before changes are made."

He saw her hand begin to tremble. She set down her wine and withdrew her hands to her lap before she continued.

"Surely you understand the way of things. I will soon be gone from here. I cannot leave my people helpless. Everything must be readied for winter. Who knows what man the king will place at Kentwood's helm? If the proper preparations are made, 'twill make for a smoother transition as the next nobleman assumes control of Kentwood."

She bit her bottom lip and lowered her eyes, steadying herself. He reached out and placed a hand over hers.

"Everything is more than ready. You have a keen eye for detail. You have left no stone unturned. And who knows? Edward may leave you in charge of Kent-wood indefinitely."

She stilled beneath his hand. She seemed so small, so defeated in that moment. He longed to sweep her into his arms and away from her troubles.

As if they had a choice.

Elizabeth's eyes, so green and usually serene, gazed into his. In them, he saw the storm clouds of uncertainty that she now lived with on a daily basis.

"We both know that is a foolish notion, Sir Gavin. I must await my fate and will go wherever the king has need of me," she continued. "My future is his to decide." She placed a hand over his and gave it a squeeze before pulling away. "But I thank you for your kind words. They are a comfort to me."

He knew she was only being realistic. Noble-women had no say in their fate, be they young brides who wed the men of their fathers choosing or widows who served as pawns on the king's political chess-board. If Edward had ventured to France with the pleasant turn of weather, he might not be bothered to answer Elizabeth's missive until late summer. If, though, the Black Prince still led the fighting in France and his father chose to remain in England, Elizabeth could have mere weeks left to manage Kentwood before the king's decision was made public.

And Gavin understood that would be the death of her spirit, for Kentwood was as much a part of her as breathing. She loved the place and its inhabitants with a nurturing passion. They were her family, her life. The cruelest blow would be when she read the king's missive instructing her to leave and hand over the property to an outsider who would claim Lord Aldred's lands and title as his own.

If only he had Edward's ear.

If Gavin were still Berwyn's acknowledged son, he might risk some type of interference. The king would be well served to leave Elizabeth at Kentwood and simply provide her with a husband in need of a title and wife. She knew the land. She knew how to make it profitable. She understood harvests and defense and held the people's loyalty. It would be extremely difficult for a stranger to come in and gain the kind of trust Elizabeth held from those at Kentwood.

But he was no longer a man of consequence in England's realm. He knew not what blood coursed through his veins. He didn't even know if Lord Aldred had kept his word and sent a missive to the king which requested that Gavin become a part of the monarch's royal guard although he thought it had occurred, based upon Lord Aldred's last moments.

As it was, Gavin found himself in limbo, and the worst kind. Not only did he have no sire and no title to claim—but he was in love.

With Elizabeth.

He didn't know how or why it began. She'd been hostile to him at the first. Gradually, though, in his short months at Kentwood, he'd come to respect her intelligence and vast knowledge of the estate. It didn't take long for him to realize she ran the property because Lord Aldred no longer could. She also had great compassion for her people and would go to any length to see them happy. He admired her spirit. Her beauty.

Every night he tried to sleep, cursing himself for ever having kissed her, for betraying the trust Lord Aldred had placed in him.

And every night he burned to touch her again, to

run his fingers through those silky tresses, to touch his mouth to hers, to possess her, body and soul.

What a foolish dream that was. Elizabeth mourned a husband who had been the best of all men. She longed to stay in her home, which would be torn from under her. Gavin, as landless as a crow, was but a wanderer.

If only he could give her Kentwood, her fondest dream...

So he hungered for the impossible, tossing and turning in his bed each night, wondering how much more he could take. Would he even have a place in Kentwood's guard, or would the new lord release him from service? Would he then choose to return to France, Elizabeth always in his thoughts, as he took enough risks on the battlefield in order to meet his death?

Gavin had soon realized that he did not wish to exist in a world where a new lord slept beside his Elizabeth each and every night, touching her sweet curves, kissing her ripe lips, knowing her in the most intimate of ways.

———

As the meal continued, Elizabeth saw the faraway look in Gavin's eyes. She wondered where his thoughts took him. Too often hers meandered back to the breaking of dawn and a kiss made of dreams. Oh, guilt was always a constant companion when she remembered her actions that morning, even with Aldred since dead and buried. While she missed her husband terribly, at times she almost convinced herself that he would have approved of a union between her and Gavin.

Her fantasies led her in the wildest of directions. Though she had childhood memories of seeing servants making love, she put her disgust aside. What if her kiss with Gavin had led to an act of love?

And what if a child had resulted?

Aldred could have claimed it as his own, without question. If the babe had been a boy, he would have been the heir to Kentwood. She would have been able to stay on, secure, raising her son to one day be lord of Kentwood and somehow marrying Gavin when Aldred passed on.

What senseless daydreams she wove, all because of one simple kiss.

Yet that kiss haunted her, both in waking and sleeping. She remembered it first thing when she awakened, and it was her last thought before sleep came. In between times, her thoughts constantly strayed to Gavin. Every day she spent time in his company, discussing the state of the soldiers and their training. She asked advice on Kentwood, rarely needing any, but simply wanting to hear his voice. It had become their habit to dine together on the dais and talk over every aspect of the estate.

She remembered how angry she'd been when he first arrived at Kentwood. Jealousy was a part of it, for he took time from Aldred that had once belonged to her. Yet, as she observed Gavin, she understood why Aldred had thought so highly of the knight. Gavin was a man to be reckoned with, physically imposing, astute, perceptive, quick-witted.

And possibly the most handsome man in all of England. She would close her eyes and relive their kiss, his hands pulling her close, his heat and passion, and find herself trembling with desire. It was something she'd never known. She'd never been interested in it, but it now haunted her.

Gavin had made her aware of this sleeping giant. All she wished was to close her eyes and be enveloped in his arms once more.

"Would you care for some cheese, my lady? More wine?"

Elizabeth rejoined reality as Gavin offered her tangible things. *If only he could offer her himself.* "Thank you, my lord. I would enjoy more of the wine."

He poured it for her and gave her the cup. She downed it in a single swallow.

He whistled low. "If only your appetite matched your thirst, my lady."

"Elizabeth," she whispered, looking into his eyes. "Please. Call me Elizabeth."

A smile played about his sensual lips. "Then if we are not to stand on ceremony, you must return the favor and call me Gavin."

"Gavin," she repeated, savoring the word she spoke. "I should like that." She longed to do more than say his name, but for now she would content herself with his company.

"Gavin," she said again, "would you be willing to accompany me as I begin my spring inspection? Aldred always insisted I take a guard of four men with me. I feel things are safe, though, about Kentwood. I must begin to examine roofs around the property, to see what repairs are needed to the cottages before the haying season begins."

She fiddled with the pocket of her cotehardie. "Would you be able to take a few days away from your men? Another trusted knight could step in and supervise. I would feel better not pulling away so many from their duties."

His answering smile warmed her down to her very toes. "Of course, Elizabeth. We may begin as early as you wish."

18

Elizabeth wished the day would never end. She had thought the same of yesterday. Gavin had accompanied her for two days now around Kentwood. They had met with the residents of every cottage and listened to their concerns. He helped her record what needed to be mended. She delighted in his easy manner with the people, and they certainly took to him. He would have made a wonderful liege lord for Kentwood.

She studied him as he spoke to Old James, the former stable master. Aldred had given the servant, up in years now, his own cottage and a bit of land to farm for his years of trusted service. Gavin spoke to Old James of his bad knee and gimpy belly and commiserated with him about their mutual dislike of peas. She had never seen Old James so charmed. She regretted that Gavin no longer had an estate to inherit, for he would have done the king proud.

"So 'tis a complete new thatched roof for you, Old James?" she asked, hoping to end their lengthy stay.

"Aye, my lady. Sir Gavin said he himself will help in making me place the envy of the land." He winked at her. "'Twill only match the envy the men now feel about me and me good looks."

She laughed. "Truly, Old James, have you come between another man and his courting of a widow?"

The bearded man smiled, his eyes crinkling in the folds of his sun-worn face. "'Tis a good thing, my lady, to get Mary's eyes cast upon me and not that surly John," he said, leaning in as he shared the confidence. "She can do much better than him, for sure. Besides, she keeps me clothes clean and food on me table."

"I trust you won't break her heart then," she proclaimed. "You have a reputation for doing so, you know."

"I do?" Old James asked innocently. He turned to Gavin. "Those who tell tales. Can't trust 'em, I say. Don't listen to a harsh word against me, my lord. I'm but a pussycat."

Gavin laughed heartily. "I have a pussycat named Homer, Old James." He pointed to where the cat sprawled in the grass behind them, soaking up the sun's rays. "He's a devil in disguise, mark my words. You may be, too, for all I know. Still," he added, "'twill be a new roof for you, ladies' man or not," and he grinned.

"Thank ye both, my lord, my lady." The old man smiled and wiped a tear. "I will go to my grave grateful that I have lived my entire life at Kentwood, that I will."

"Let's not make it an early grave, Old James," she teased. "I would hope you would stay around long enough to enjoy your new roof."

She motioned to Gavin. "Come, my lord. We still have a few places to visit this day. Good day to you, Old James. And tell Mary hello."

Old James guffawed loudly and waved goodbye to them.

As they walked their horses down the road, Homer trailing them, Gavin shook his head. "He is most flirtatious with the ladies, in truth?"

She nodded. "He might have nary a hair atop his head and a good many teeth missing, but Old James is winsome, is he not?"

Gavin agreed. "I hope to be charming the ladies when I am his age. He looks as if he still has a great deal of fun."

"That he does," she replied, but her words were drowned out by a loud thunderclap. She turned her eyes up and scanned the heavens. "I had not realized how the sky darkened, thanks to how entertaining Old James was."

Gavin glanced up. "'Twill storm any minute now." He pointed ahead of them. "I see Homer has already made his run for shelter. Shall we hasten back to Old James' place, or is there somewhere closer we can ride out the rain?"

She thought a moment. "Around the curve there is a small cottage no longer in use. It belonged to Old James' cousin, which is why Aldred gave him the cottage he did. The poor man died two days after Old James moved in. It has been vacant ever since."

Drops of rain began to pelt them. "Then we'd best make a dash for it," he said. "Come on."

They spurred their horses to a full gallop. Great sheets of rain stung them as the skies opened up. They scurried to the edge of a wooded area.

"There!" she cried. "'Tis but a stone's throw ahead."

They raced the last bit and tethered their horses before running to the cottage. Gavin threw open the door, and Elizabeth rushed in, out of breath, Homer darting past her. He stepped in and closed the door. A lone, dirty window stood next to the door. Gavin went and peered out.

"Hopefully 'twill not last too long." He turned and looked over the mostly bare room. "At least there's a chair apiece. Come, Elizabeth, let us sit and rest a spell."

She moved to sit upon one of the chairs. Her teeth began to chatter. Embarrassed, she raised a hand to her mouth and covered it. She locked her jaw, hoping to cease the chatter.

"You are cold," he said as he pulled the remaining chair close to her.

"Oh, 'tis not so bad," she said, a shiver betraying her.

He looked about. "Here, drag your chair over to the fireplace. There are a few logs next to it. I can start a fire. You will be warmed in no time."

Elizabeth watched as he quickly got a blaze going. She stood and moved closer to it, resting her hands against the stone as she leaned into the heat. They'd been gone for most of the day, and she hadn't realized how tired she'd grown.

"You shake still," Gavin said quietly. He moved behind her and placed his hands upon her shoulders. He began to rub her arms in his hands, slowly gliding up and down. His fingers held such heat in them. Indeed, his very closeness seemed a stronger blaze than that in the grate before her.

Without thinking, she leaned back into him, absorbing the warmth that he possessed, even in his wet tunic.

Then his arms slid round her waist, drawing her against him. Her breath caught in her throat at his very nearness. His fingers locked, trapping her in the circle of his arms.

"Gavin?" she asked, afraid to move, afraid to break the magic spell. She'd longed to be right where she now stood. Her pounding heart betrayed her fear at their situation.

His response was wordless, but one she treasured, nonetheless. He bent and kissed her ear, his hot breath sending shivers down her spine. His lips moved to her neck, scorching a path there, before they touched her cheek.

One arm held her tightly against him as his other palm moved to caress her breast. Elizabeth moaned. Her knees turned liquid. If Gavin had not held her, she would have puddled on the floor.

He slipped a hand into the side slit of her cote-hardie and touched her breast again. This time the heat of his palm was even closer. Her heart pounded and that strange throbbing she'd felt before, when he'd kissed her, began in earnest. His fingers played with her nipple through her under-tunic and chemise, teasing it to a taut peak.

She thought she would faint from the pleasure. He moved his hand to the other breast, lavishing just as much attention on it as the first, all the while pressing hot kisses along her throat and cheek. She leaned harder into him, her head falling back as the throbbing between her legs became almost painful.

Suddenly, he spun her in his arms. She clung to him wildly. Her fingers dug into his arms. His hands splayed along her back. His mouth was everywhere, in her hair, on her eyelids, her cheeks, the tip of her nose, her mouth.

His heated kisses overwhelmed her. She couldn't breathe. And yet they continued, his mouth insistent on hers. Her lips parted, allowing his tongue entrance, and she welcomed it. He stroked her with it, a constant, dizzying motion that kept her head spinning. Her senses filled with him, his scent, his touch, his taste. Tears began to flow down her cheeks.

That stopped him.

Gavin lifted his mouth from hers. "Elizabeth?" he asked. "Have I hurt you?" He held her at arm's length and studied her.

The concern in his eyes touched her very core. "No," she whispered. "'Twas just so beautiful... I... had to cry."

He smiled, a heartbreaking smile, and caught her up in his arms again. "No, my love, you are the beautiful one." He kissed her gently, tenderly. The passion was still there, but it was more controlled now.

She hiccupped.

He drew back, a questioning look on his face. She felt the heat of her blush and hiccupped again.

"I... I sometimes hiccup when I cry," she explained. "I didn't mean to ruin things."

Gavin laughed and kissed her brow. "Oh, Elizabeth, only you would cry and hiccup when a man wished to make love to you."

Her eyes widened. "You... you wish to make love to me?"

He cupped her cheek. "More than anything in the world." He kissed her lips tenderly. "More than you could ever imagine."

She smiled shyly at him. "That would be... nice." She hiccupped again.

"Nice?" he asked. "Nice?" He brushed his lips against hers. "Oh, my lady, nice is not the word that comes to mind. Nice brings pictures of a row of colorful poppies or the taste of a sweet apple tart. A pleasant song or a chore completed."

He smiled wickedly at her. "What I had in mind was not exactly... nice. 'Twill be better than nice, I assure you."

His hands slipped down her back, his fingers curling around her bottom, drawing her closer even as his mouth took hers by storm. She found her fingers entangled in his hair, the breathlessness overwhelming her again as his kisses made all rational thought flee.

She agreed that *nice* had not been the exact word she was looking for.

Gavin swept her into his arms. Hers went around his neck and she kissed him for the first time, making her own bold move. His growl let her know he approved. He broke the kiss and looked around the room.

"I see no bed, my lady. The straw on the floor 'twill have to suffice. But," he said, his eyes glowing at her, "I guarantee you won't notice the difference."

He carried her to the corner of the room. As he placed her on the straw, she raised a hand to his chest. His heart beat as fast as hers did. Oh, God in Heaven, she wanted this man!

A voice from outside invaded her thoughts.

"Elizabeth? Gavin? Are you there?"

19

Gavin stood quickly as Elizabeth gasped.

"'Tis Robert!" she said, scrambling to her feet.

Gavin took in her lush mouth, swollen from his kisses. "Face the fire. Act as though you're warming yourself. Don't turn to look Robert in the eye. He'll guess at once what mischief we've been up to. He may already know."

He strode to the door as a shadow darkened the window. He threw open the door and smiled.

"Hello, Robert. Out for a ride in the rain?"

His friend looked at him questioningly as he stepped into the small room. Gavin saw Elizabeth now stood before the fire, her arms wrapped about her, Homer rubbing against her leg.

"Good day to you, Robert," she replied, all traces of her hiccups now vanished. She turned her head slightly. "You may want to share in the fire Sir Gavin built. I swear 'tis soaked to the skin, I am, and chilled to my bones." She gazed back at the fire and held her hands out to its warmth.

Gavin closed the door, noting the storm had let up considerably.

"I was on my way to Kentwood when it suddenly hit," Robert replied. "I rode a quarter league and called in upon Old James, who graciously allowed me to take shelter in his cottage."

"We just came from there ourselves," Gavin said. "He's quite an interesting character."

Robert headed toward the fire. "That he is." He went and stood next to Elizabeth. "Old James said you'd called there not a quarter hour before I arrived."

Elizabeth continued to stare into the fire. "Yes, Sir Gavin accompanied me today on my rounds, visiting each cottage and its residents. You know how I like to have all repairs done before summer arrives and prefer to see what needs to be done in person."

"And you had time to do so, my friend?" Robert asked. Suspicion rose in his eyes as he spoke. "With better weather at hand, the king will be demanding additional troops for his war. I would think you would be busy preparing those men—or have you forgotten what war is like?"

Gavin held his temper. Robert baited him. Had his friend guessed at what had occurred between Elizabeth and him only moments ago? Part, too, came from guilt. Although Robert had made no formal declaration to him, he knew his friend well enough to suspect he was also in love with Elizabeth.

Did Robert have earlier suspicions about their relationship? Was that why he sought them out after learning they were nearby? With Aldred now dead, would Robert plan to petition King Edward to make Elizabeth his bride and join their properties together? Or had he already done so on the sly and simply awaited word from the king? He would be a fool not to try.

Gavin smiled pleasantly, pushing aside the

sudden hostility he experienced toward his old friend.

"I have left a most capable knight is in charge today, one who was second in command when Rufus was captain of the guard. I gather the men were ready for a respite, as hard as I have driven them these past few weeks. By accompanying Elizabeth myself on her errands, it saved me from providing a guard of men better left to their exercises." Gavin leaned against the door. "What brings you to Kentwood in such inclement weather?"

"An invitation." Robert turned to Elizabeth. "My father wished to express his condolences to you in person. He was far too ill to attend Lord Aldred's funeral mass and burial, but he would have you come to Fondren and visit with him."

She nodded. "I would very much like to spend time with Lord Markham. 'Tis been far too long since I last saw him."

"Then 'tis agreed. Would you come for supper tonight? You may stay the night, and I shall see you returned to Kentwood early on the morrow."

Gavin's instant protest died on his lips. Who was he to tell Elizabeth what she could and could not do? Robert and his father were her equal. He, on the other hand, was but captain of Kentwood's guard, a man of little consequence in the eyes of nobility.

And one jealous to the very bone that Robert would be with the woman Gavin now knew that he truly loved.

Elizabeth faced Robert. "I would be happy to accompany you back to Fondren this eve." She fingered her clothing. "'Tis a mess I am, though. Mayhap I can return to Kentwood and change beforehand. I would hate to frighten Lord Markham with such a bedraggled appearance."

She smiled at Robert, who took her hand. "Come, then. We're a ways from Kentwood. Let us ride there now since the storm has passed on."

She frowned. "I had wanted to visit a few more tenants this day."

Gavin looked at her. "How many more cottages are left to see?"

She thought a moment. "If I return early on the morn and you can attend me again, my visits will be complete by early afternoon. Is that convenient for you, Sir Gavin?"

He saw a tenderness in her eyes as she looked at him and had to tamp down the stir of desire he felt.

"Of course, my lady. What is agreeable to you is to me, as well."

"Then shall we venture out?" Robert inquired. "'Tis certain the rain has now stopped."

Gavin reached down and scooped up Homer, who yowled in protest of leaving the fire's warmth. He slipped the growing cat into his sack and doused the fire.

The trio exited the abandoned cottage and untied their horses. Robert's hands quickly and possessively went to Elizabeth's waist. He lifted her into the saddle before he swung up into his own. Gavin remounted his horse and kept a pleasant look upon his face as he boiled inside.

They ventured back to Kentwood in silence. Gavin struggled to tame the waves of jealousy that flooded him every time he looked at Robert.

———

Elizabeth waved away the servant. "I am ready to burst, I fear," she joked, "but I thank you all the same." She looked to Lord Markham. "You truly outdid yourself, my lord. What a sumptuous feast! I expected but a quiet supper."

The nobleman's smile trembled, as did the hand he placed over hers. The constant shaking had set upon him nigh on three years ago. It pained her to see him suffer so.

"Anything for you, my girl," he replied. "I feel honored you would come and see me." He frowned, and she knew he concentrated on his words. He seemed to have a hard time getting them out at times. "I was saddened to hear of Aldred's passing. I know you miss him a great deal."

"Indeed I do, my lord." Her eyes filled with tears and she blinked hard to hold them back. "My lord husband was a good man. He is missed by many."

"But you still have a long life ahead of you, my lady. I hope it 'twill be a happy one. One with the right man." Lord Markham smiled and looked over at his son. "Robert is a good man, too."

"Yes," she replied, hesitating a moment as the pieces suddenly fell into place. Did Lord Markham think she would marry Robert? Was this why he requested her to visit? Yes, she cared about Robert, but she saw herself with no man.

None except Gavin, that is.

And that could never come to pass. The king would exchange the freedom she now knew for a prison with some favored nobleman. Kentwood would be a jewel given to another courtier that pleased Edward, one who had helped England to victory in a battle against her nemesis, or simply a man who made Edward smile for a moment or two. She was but a pawn in a political game of favorites, powerless to sway the king's opinion as to her preference.

Wouldn't Edward laugh to learn he whom she truly wanted to wed was a bastard knight, one who had no idea as to his father's identity? When she, Elizabeth of Aldwyn, had been married to one of the leading noblemen in the kingdom. She lived on one of the most prestigious estates in England, yet now she longed for a penniless knight that would be seen as having no real worth in the eyes of many.

Lord Markham patted her hand. "I grow weak, I'm afraid," he told her. "I must retire for the night. Will I have the pleasure of seeing you on the morrow, my child?"

She took in his pale skin and glassy eyes and shot Robert a look. He immediately headed their way. "Nay, my lord, I must return to Kentwood very early tomorrow, for I have tenants to visit. Mayhap we can visit again sometime soon."

"Yes, of course." Markham looked to his son. "I tire, my boy."

Robert gestured to two servants hovering nearby. "Please see my father to his solar." He leaned down and kissed the old man's cheek. "Goodnight, Father. Sleep well."

They watched as the men helped their liege lord from the room.

Robert turned and smiled at her. "Thank you for putting up with an old man's ramblings. He thinks the world of you, Elizabeth." Robert took a sip of wine from the cup he carried. "Would you care to adjourn to my study? We can have a quieter conversation there."

She decided to do so. If Lord Markham had put any

notions into Robert's head of their marrying, she wanted them dispelled. Now. While she treasured her friendship with Robert, she looked upon him as an older sibling. Coupling with him would seem like a sin.

She followed him down the corridor to the small room. A fire burned in the grate. A chessboard sat on a small table, its pieces ready for two players. Nearby was a carafe of wine and two cups, along with a wedge of cheese and some apples. Elizabeth had no doubt Robert was up to something.

He ushered her in and closed the door behind him. "Would you care to match wits?" He motioned to the chessboard.

"No, thank you. I am rather tired from making the rounds of the estate these past few days. I fear my concentration would not do justice to our game. Mayhap another time."

She sat in one of the chairs by the game board, though. Robert ambled over and stood with his back to the fire.

"There's wine if you'd like some."

"No, I have had my share of food and drink for to-day. You have been a most excellent host."

A silence fell between them. She studied her hands lying in her lap. She'd never experienced being uncomfortable in Robert's company before. She thought it possible she had misread the situation entirely. If so, she was being grossly unfair to her good friend.

"Elizabeth?"

Robert's voice interrupted her thoughts. She looked to him and saw a longing on his face. After having been with Gavin, she could not mistake it. Had she been blind all these years? When did Robert gain an affection for her? Had it always been there, hidden away until Aldred was gone?

More importantly, how would she handle it now?

"Yes, Robert?" She tried to still her heart, which beat uncomfortably against her ribs.

He stepped away from the fire and sat across from her. "I would speak to you about something of great consequence. Something that might take you by surprise."

She decided not to mince words. "That you fancy yourself in love with me and wish us to wed?"

His jaw dropped, and then a brilliant smile stole across his features. He swept chess pieces from the board and reached across to take her hands in his.

"Oh, my dearest one, I had no idea that you knew. I was to keep silent but have been eager to share my devotion to you."

She narrowed her eyes. "What do you mean? Keep silent?"

He chuckled. "I thought perhaps Aldred changed his mind and spoke to you after all."

"Told me what?" She cocked her head to one side. "Of what do you speak, Robert?"

He studied her, a solemn look now upon his face. "Then he did not, as we had agreed." He gave her hands a squeeze. "Before he died, Lord Aldred and I discussed your future."

Anger swept through her. "You deliberated my future? Did either of you think to include me in such discussions?" Her tone was sharp as she withdrew her hands from his.

"Oh, Elizabeth, you know how Aldred worshipped the very ground you trod upon. He only wanted to see you adequately cared for when he was gone."

She crossed her arms in front of her. "I see. And you are the one appointed to care for me?"

He smiled. "'Tis only natural, Elizabeth. I've been in love with you from the moment I laid eyes upon you, years and years ago."

"But," she stammered, "what of your betrothed? The one who died of plague? I thought you carried such strong memories of her. You would choose never to marry because of her. You told me so yourself."

"Do you think I could reveal to you how I felt?" He stood. "I can see how you would be confused. You were married to Aldred. I was betrothed to another. When she died, I gave thanks to God in His Heaven. I led everyone to believe I mourned deeply for her, when she was but little more than a stranger to me."

He paused and gazed at her with an intensity that frightened her. "You are the only one I have loved, Elizabeth. I knew the day would come when Aldred would no longer stand between us. When he told me a marriage between the two of us was the very thing he had in mind, I could have wept tears of joy."

She stood and began pacing the small room. "So the two of you decided what my life would be, without regard as to how I felt? You plotted and schemed? Did you ever think the king might be averse to your plans?"

He came and stood before her, grasping her elbows in his hands. "Aldred wrote to King Edward before his death, asking that the king consider our marriage and the joining of our estates, in part as a show of respect for Aldred's many years of good service to the crown. He felt certain that Edward would look favorably upon such a wise union."

She started to pull away, but Robert held fast to her. "Elizabeth, you need never leave Kentwood. We can live there the rest of our lives. You will be safe and not bartered about. I will show you love and devotion like no man has ever shown a woman. I love you, Elizabeth dearest. I will do whatever it takes to make you happy."

She shook her head from side to side in refusal, her fists balled at her sides. "But Aldred said his letter was to ask the king to allow Gavin a place in his royal guard. I saw it, Robert. Aldred would not have lied to me. I knew him too well. I would have known of such a scheme."

Robert shook her gently. "Listen to me, Elizabeth. He gave the letter to me. He refused to have you to worry about him. He knew how it saddened you when he spoke of his ill health. I sent the *courlieu* myself. The missive had Aldred's seal, but it was my messenger that reached the king."

He sighed. "'Tis sorry I am that this has taken you by surprise. I am sure Aldred did write to the king of Gavin, whatever the case might be. Gavin's been so secretive since he arrived, nothing like he was in the old days. I cannot understand why he will not simply return home to Ashgrove. Why does he insist upon hanging about Kentwood, acting as head of the guard when one day he will inherit Ashgrove? Why does he wish a place among Edward's household?"

Her temper flared, but she reigned it in, not wanting to betray the history of Gavin's two years of imprisonment in France and rejection by his father. Instead, she dropped further discussion of Gavin and returned to the problem at hand.

"'Tis more than surprise I feel now, Robert. 'Tis anger. I am furious that you and Aldred plotted with the king behind my back."

He gave her a sobering look. "You could very well

go to a stranger, Elizabeth. The king may marry you off to whomever he chooses. Think, would you? You are an intelligent woman. I offer you a life that you have known, in a place that you love, with people who adore you. I have loved you for years and kept my distance and my silence, but now I will speak and be heard. I want you, Elizabeth. You *and* Kentwood. 'Tis within my grasp. Aldred believed King Edward would allow you the time he asked for, so you could adjust to this idea."

She straightened her spine, her chin rising. "Did you not think I should have a hand in what happened? You and Aldred treat me as a child. I am a woman, Robert, a strong-willed woman who will—"

He grabbed her by the shoulders, his fingers painfully keeping her in place. "We can be happy together, you and I. I know it. You will grow to love me. I have never been more certain of anything."

Robert pressed his lips to hers. Elizabeth squirmed, turning her face away from the unwanted kiss. When she finally met his gaze, he was no longer the charming man she had known for so many years, the one who'd been like the brother she'd never had. A maniacal light glowed in his eyes. It frightened her.

He took her face between his palms and forced another kiss upon her, holding her still under his grasp. She chose not to fight him this time. She went totally still instead, numbed by all that had occurred.

When he finished, she raised her gaze to his. He looked down upon her, a satisfied smile tugging at the corners of his mouth. "We are meant to be together, Elizabeth. You shall see."

20

Gavin pondered Elizabeth's silence. Every time they reached a tenant's cottage, she was all smiles and courteous charm. The minute they left, however, she fell mute. So far, he hadn't asked what was wrong. He sensed she would tell him in good time.

Something troubled her, though. He thought it had to do with Robert's father. Mayhap seeing the man in such ill health brought back a painful reminder of Aldred's last days. Still, Gavin hoped she would shake off these feelings. They had so little time to spend together, alone in this way. With a castle full of people, he couldn't fathom another way of being alone with her after they completed their rounds today.

Unless he was the problem.

Did she regret the kisses they had shared, his caresses along her sweet curves? Did the idea of making love with him displease her? Had he read more into the feelings he had supposed she held for him?

True, neither had spoken with words, but he thought her body responded to his touch as if she truly cared for him. Why was she now distancing herself from him? Had she settled into the idea that he was not to be her fate? Mayhap fear of becoming with child before going to another husband troubled her. If that were the case, he could understand her reluctance.

Time drew to a close, and they visited the last cottage on Kentwood land. He walked his horse beside hers, as close as he dared without actually touching her as they made their way back to the castle proper.

It was torture, pure and simple.

"I wish to speak to you, my lord."

Elizabeth's voice startled him, as she'd not addressed him at all this day. It was stiff, formal, with none of the emotion he longed to hear. Gavin steeled himself for her words, even as he craved to cut them short with a sweet kiss.

"Would you care to discuss it now, my lady?"

She halted her mount in the road, her eyes anxious. "I would prefer that, yes." She hesitated. "We are not far from the cottage we stopped at yesterday. I would like to rest there."

She bit down on her full, bottom lip and spurred her horse into a trot. Her behavior puzzled him. To go to the cottage, they would truly be isolated, not in the open. Dare he hope she wanted to speak with her lips and not with words?

They arrived and entered much as the last time. Homer chose to scamper outside near their tethered horses. The spring day had turned warm, so he did not offer to build a fire. Elizabeth went and sat upon the same chair as before. He took the one next to her.

Immediately, she sprang up and started pacing the small room. Gavin let her take her time. He knew she would speak when ready.

Finally, she marched and stood in front of him. As

he looked up at her, he saw tears welling in her magnificent green eyes. Elizabeth did not seem a woman who shed them lightly. He reached for her hand, linking his fingers with hers. She clutched him tightly, holding on as if her very life depended upon it.

"My lady?"

A sob escaped, and he immediately pulled her into his lap. He stroked her hair, whispering softly to her, trying to reassure her, not knowing what ailed her so.

Finally, the tears subsided. She lifted her head from his chest and studied his face intently, as if she wished to memorize it.

"Tell me we can be together, Gavin. Tell me we could run away, just the two of us. Leave Kentwood and its inhabitants behind. No thought as to the consequences."

His arms tightened about her. "I wish I could grant such a request, sweetheart, but I fear the king would have my head upon a platter when he caught up to us. Marrying without his permission would only be the start of our woes."

He had not shared with her why he had arrived at Kentwood and thought he owed her an explanation now.

"I was brought up a nobleman's son in the north country, an only child to an overbearing father and a mother who smothered me with kisses and then disappeared for days at a time, lost in her prayers. My happiest times were fostering at Kentwood with Lord Aldred and fighting alongside him in France. When Robert and I fell captive in battle, Lord Markham sent the requested ransoming, freeing Robert to return home."

He swallowed hard. "My father refused to pay the ransom that would win me my freedom. I cannot tell you how I questioned his decision to abandon me to my captors' contempt."

Her hand stroked the side of his face. Her touch and knowing he could never truly be one with her left a bitter taste in his mouth.

Her voice soft, she asked, "What happened, Gavin?"

"When I escaped, I returned to my home, only to find my mother dead and my father remarried. He informed me that I was not his son. My mother got herself with child by another man. Berwyn said he would kill me if I returned to Ashgrove ever again. Having nowhere else to go, I turned to Lord Aldred, the one man I trusted with my life."

Gavin took her hand from his face and kissed her open palm tenderly. "I have nothing to offer you, sweetest Elizabeth. No estate. Not even my good name, for I have not a clue who my sire was. We can never be, my love. I was selfish to express my longings to you yesterday. You must go to whomever the king sends you, for it could never be me."

Pain was written across her brow. "Even if that man is Robert? Would you see me with your dearest friend, Gavin? Imagine me lying in his arms? Bearing his children? Knowing 'tis you I want above all others, and that I die inside more each day I am separated from you?"

The image she created forced the breath from him, sure as he'd been punched in his gut. It was easier to envision her going to a faceless man in a nameless place, but not to the very next estate, where her body would be worshipped by his most treasured companion.

"No," he whispered. "It cannot be."

Elizabeth bit her lip, her eyes squeezing closed. "Yes," she replied. "Robert informed me he and Aldred planned it without my knowledge. That Aldred wrote to the king and asked him to consider the request of Robert becoming my husband and uniting the two properties once Aldred died."

She opened her eyes, and Gavin saw the sheer desperation in them. "King Edward thought the world of Aldred. He is sure to grant a dying man's wish." She leaned forward and rested her forehead against his. "And I cannot imagine a life with Robert, at Kentwood, only to pass you, day after day, at the head of the guard."

Her tears began to flow again. "I hunger so for you, Gavin. I cannot live if I am not with you."

Her hiccups began again, bringing a smile to his tormented soul. He should remove himself from her presence now, leave Kentwood immediately, yet her body pressed closer to his, like a siren's song he was helpless to command.

He touched his fingers to her cheeks, brushing away the tears that fell against porcelain skin. Slowly, he brought his mouth to hers, brushing it ever so gently. He felt her tremble at his touch. He stood, with her in his arms, and once more placed her upon the bed of straw in the corner of the tiny room. She looked up at him with such trusting eyes, he felt his own moisten as he bent over her.

"I love you," he said, his thumbs tracing her eyebrows, smoothing them. He ran his hands along her face and cradled it gently between them. "I would make you a part of me, Elizabeth. A part that can never belong to Robert. 'Twill only be mine."

"Yes," she whispered, pulling him down to her.

Gavin kissed her slowly, wanting to savor this moment in time, mayhap the only one they would ever again spend alone.

———

The world ceased to exist as he deepened the kiss. Elizabeth sighed at his touch. The hands that stroked her ignited a fire within her. She didn't care if it blazed out of control. Normally, she would think ahead, worry about the consequences of such foolish actions. For once, though, consequences be damned. She was with the most beautiful man in the world, a man who'd just proclaimed his love for her.

She chose to speak from her heart. "I love you, Gavin. I do love you so."

She pushed her fingers into his raven locks, stroked his muscled chest, longed to make him purr as his little cat Homer did. His hands were everywhere, calling out to her, searing her with his touch.

"I wish I had sweet words of poetry to tell you how your beauty affects me," he told her, nuzzling her neck. "I always thought poets silly creatures, raving about a woman's looks, but I find I have no words to do you justice now."

"Oh, Gavin," she replied. "You are a painter, my love, and I your canvas. Let your hands be the brush that tells our tale."

He lifted her garments from her, one by one, until she lay naked against the straw. His eyes told her he approved of what he saw. Quickly, he doffed his own clothes and held her against him, spreading his tunic between her and the rough straw.

Then he kissed her again, more gently than ever before. Slowly, his lips slid from her mouth, trailing down her throat and to her breast. He flicked a tongue across the nipple, teasing it into a peak, before he did the same with the other. Elizabeth cried out in pure joy, the feelings so new and pleasurable.

As he suckled her breast, his hand slid along her thigh. Strong fingers stroked up and down as his knee nudged her legs apart. She fought a sense of panic that struck her. Remembered images from her childhood danced before her eyes.

"Relax, sweetheart. 'Tis only me," he said.

She forced herself to breathe deeply, to trust this man she'd known for only two months but wished she could devote a lifetime to. His kisses distracted her, causing her to lose her fear.

Then he touched her in the most intimate of spots. A rush of air escaped her lips. Was the kind of pleasure he brought not forbidden? Did a woman allow such a thing to occur?

All rational thought was cast aside as he eased a finger into her and began to slowly move it in and out, back and forth. Her hands grasped the straw by her side, kneading it like a kitten at his mother's teat.

"Yes, love, you're ready for me," he crooned, his strokes growing bolder and more rapid. "Come to me, sweetest Elizabeth. Enjoy."

She rose now to meet each stroke, her hips lifting off the ground. The throbbing caused her blood to sing, boiling into a sweet ecstasy. Her head thrashed from side to side as a pressure within her built. Suddenly, an explosion of stars blinded her, and her body quivered violently against his hand.

"Oh, God, what have you done?" Her breathing was rapid and shallow. She clung to Gavin, who kissed her again and again.

Then his body covered hers, and she reveled in his

hard muscles against her soft curves. The hairs on his chest tickled her bare breasts. His scent, a mixture of soap and horse and male, became her scent. She wrapped her arms about his neck, wanting him closer to her.

But something replaced his hand. It began filling her, stretching her. It was too much. It hurt. The panic began again. She tried to cry out, but her words were swallowed in his kisses. She began to struggle as he thrust hard, and a sharp pain became her only focus.

He tore his lips from hers. "God's wounds, Elizabeth! You are a virgin!"

The pain already subsided, but a new one replaced it as he pulled away from her. She clutched at him.

"Please, Gavin, no, don't leave me. I need you. Stay with me."

He leaned back toward her, his nearness comforting her again. "Oh, dearest," he said, stroking her hair, "if only I had known. I could have been gentler."

"No," she answered, "you would not have touched me. At all." The look in his eyes told her that her assumption was correct. "I love you, Gavin. I want you. I need you. Come back to me. Please." Her voice broke.

She saw him fight something within him. She brushed a finger along his lower lip. His mouth parted and nibbled on it playfully. Elizabeth knew with that gesture she had won.

Gavin entered her again slowly. This time she understood what was happening. The pain was no more. In its place was a fullness, a richness. As he began to move against her, she instinctively understood what to do. She began to move with him, in time to the rhythm of the throb's return. Their dance grew more frantic, Gavin's kisses more potent.

Then she cried out, a pleasure so great rippling through her that she neither understood nor questioned it but simply rode out the waves of passion. He shuddered against her and collapsed, his breathing ragged in her ear. He rolled to his side and brought her even closer.

"Never was love so sweet as this," he told her. "In my wildest imaginings, never have I been so moved by the touch of a woman." He brushed back a stray lock from her face. "Oh, my dearest, sweetest love." He cradled her tenderly in his arms, his cheek next to hers.

For Elizabeth, no words came. She only knew now, this moment, and the heat and love that radiated between them.

Tomorrow—and Robert—could wait.

21

Gavin looked over the yard, pleased with the swordplay that took place. If Lord Aldred had sent his best men to fight for the king in France last year, he was certain this new crop of trained soldiers destined to join them would do Kentwood proud.

He wondered for the hundredth time if he should go with them when they left in a fortnight for France. A week had passed since Elizabeth shared with him Aldred's plans for her and Robert to wed. She had received no word from King Edward yet, but that brief lull would change soon enough.

They had spent no time alone since making love, yet he still could feel the touch of her hands upon his chest, her nails raking sensually along his back. Thoughts of Elizabeth filled every day and even his dreams at night. He constantly tried to force them aside in order to pay attention to the tasks at hand.

Robert hadn't called at Kentwood during this interlude. Gavin didn't trust himself to see his friend again. In a matter of time, Robert would more than likely have King Edward's permission to take Elizabeth to wife and become master of both her and Kentwood.

He'd once been certain that he would die for Robert in combat. Gavin still knew he would if Robert's life was endangered. But now a woman stood between them. Gavin could offer an intimate friendship to his comrade no longer. It already tormented him enough to know that most likely, Elizabeth would soon be Robert's to possess.

In that moment, he realized he must return to France. No other choice remained. He would rather die a brave death on the battlefield and honor his king and country than see piece by piece of him wither away and die every day by staying at Kentwood. That was his fate if he chose to remain and watch another man with his Elizabeth. Staying would become a worse hell than the prison he had existed in while being held captive in France. If his life were to be hell on earth, he would prefer one of his own choosing.

He would tell her of his decision tonight. She would try and talk him out of it, but he had made up his mind. The answer had been before him all along. He simply hadn't wanted to admit it, for it meant leaving Elizabeth behind. Still, it was the honorable thing to do. She would miss him, but she loved her life at Kentwood. She would stay busy and as time passed, memories of him would slowly dim.

She would have children, he supposed. He remembered his surprise in finding her to still be a virgin. They didn't speak of it afterward. He thought of all those lonely years that Aldred must not have been able to perform his marital duty for his wife. Elizabeth was yet young enough to provide Robert with an heir. She would be a good mother, the best.

It was inevitable. He must go. He would tell her. Tonight.

———

Three days passed before Gavin's chance came. Elizabeth rushed to deliver a child the night he intended to make her aware of his decision to leave with the Kentwood men bound for the war in France. The second night she nursed Nelia's nephew. The boy came down with a sudden fever, and Elizabeth spent all day and night with him before it broke.

By the third day, he despaired when told Elizabeth met with the ladies of Kentwood in preparation for the next day's May Day celebration. Nelia scolded him as he tried to interrupt their planning.

"You must know, Sir Gavin, that there are sashes being sewn and wreaths created to wear in the women's hair. Lady Elizabeth must approve the final list for the games to be played and arrange the dyeing of the trenchers. All foods must be green, you know, in honor of May Day."

The old servant's eyes gleamed. "The feast will be wonderful, of course. Lady Elizabeth outdoes herself each year. The people cannot imagine what new, creative ideas she will come up with for tomorrow's play."

He glumly retreated to the barracks, where Homer curled up and fell asleep on his bed. His burden lay heavily upon him. He wished the ships sailed for France tonight. He would choose to be a coward and not even tell Elizabeth goodbye. The idea of parting from her caused him a physical pain. He'd teased other men countless times when they spoke of being in love. Now he knew what suffering they had endured.

A clear day full of sunshine and few clouds marked the May Day celebration at Kentwood the next morn. Gavin partook in wearing a green sash across his chest and dancing around the maypole counterclockwise, singing as loudly as the next man. He had determined to enjoy this celebration, which would most likely be his last May Day. No regrets would cloud today.

All day, though, his eyes never strayed far from his love. Her eyes sparkled at the fun, and the green from her tunic and sash made her green eyes sparkle even greener. She helped judge the May Queen contest alongside him and Cedd. Gavin thought Elizabeth the most beautiful woman there, but Cedd told him she refused to be considered for the title each year. Instead, they awarded it to a young girl of six-and-ten, with roses blooming on her cheeks and long, fair hair unbound to her waist. Despite her youth and beauty, he thought Elizabeth's face far more comely than the new May Queen's.

The afternoon saw a bevy of games and contests held. He watched from the sidelines, amused by the exuberance the residents of Kentwood expressed. He helped in collecting greenery to make wreaths to adorn the great hall and then joined in the stamping dance that completed the outdoor activities.

Feasting in the great hall went on for hours. The mistress of Kentwood also provided entertainment while the meal progressed, as strolling musicians and jugglers performed. Even a man with a small dog who did tricks caused great cheers to go up every minute or two. The merry atmosphere became louder as keg after keg of ale was consumed.

Gavin knew his men would be exhausted tomorrow and decided to tell Rufus to let them sleep in an extra hour or two. Training exercises would be light, as he knew more than a few heads would be heavy. He rose to find Rufus and pass along the word when he saw Robert enter the great hall at the far side of the room. He didn't know if Elizabeth had invited him to the festivities, but he had no need of idle conversation with his friend.

He looked for a way to avoid Robert and skirted the edges of the room. As he passed Rufus, a wench on his lap, Gavin paused, placing a hand on the soldier's shoulder.

"Rufus, I think it would do the men good to sleep in a bit tomorrow." He had to bark out his words, so great was the noise in the hall.

"Aye, Gavin, 'twill be much appreciated. Figure in time to soak a few heads in the cold trough, too. Mine included."

He nodded and continued to edge about the room. He reached the doors to the great hall and almost slipped out when a hand brushed his sleeve. Turning, he saw Robert standing there.

"A fine May Day to you, Gavin."

He nodded curtly. "The same to you, my friend. Excuse me, I have business I must attend to. Please, go and enjoy yourself. And try to sample some of the pear tarts. I know what a sweet tooth you have."

He smiled, hoping the small talk would satisfy Robert, and left the noisy room. He walked briskly down the corridor, thinking he would return to the barracks. As he stepped out from the keep, however, the cool spring air tempted him. He decided to head to the stables. He hadn't been riding at night for ages. It would be just the thing to clear his head.

He cut across the bailey and stepped inside the stables. All was quiet. Every man, down to the smallest stable hand, must be celebrating tonight. It made him feel old and alone. He lit a lantern and took but a few steps when he heard his name.

"Gavin!" The urgent whisper carried through the stable. It could be but one person. His heart beat rapidly as he turned.

"Elizabeth."

She stood in the doorway, a silhouette against the night sky behind her. The ache that seemed a part of his every waking minute pushed heavily against his heart.

"I saw you leave," she said and walked toward him. "I have had no chance to speak to you in days." She came to stand before him, a vision of loveliness.

She placed a hand upon his arm. "I've missed you." He heard the wistfulness in her voice.

"And I, you," he replied. "We must talk. I've come to a decision."

She placed a finger against his lips. "No talk tonight. I see something in your eyes, Gavin. I know I will not like what you have to say."

He wrapped a hand about hers and brushed his lips against its velvet softness. "No, Elizabeth. We might not have another moment like this one again."

A glowing smile lit her face. "I know. 'Tis why I forbid any further talk. Save that for later. This is what I have wanted to do for days."

She touched her palm to his face and held it there. Just her simple caress caused him to burn with desire. He bent and covered her mouth with his. His arms came about her and drew her near.

Oh, how she fit so well against him, as if God made her just for him. He loved this woman more than life itself. But this could go on no longer. He had to give her her freedom. In doing so, he must push her away.

Gavin broke the kiss. He swallowed hard and forced out the words.

"I am leaving, Elizabeth. I shall accompany the men who depart for France in ten days' time."

"No!" she gasped, gripping her hands round his arms, her nails digging in. "'Tis impossible. I cannot let you go."

"You must," he told her. "'Tis best for all. Soon the king will give his orders. We both know you will be expected to marry Robert, just as Lord Aldred requested. Uniting Kentwood and Fondren is a perfect plan, one King Edward will favor. And I cannot watch from a distance, my love. I still love Robert like a brother, but I cannot see you by his side. Knowing the liberties he will take with you is more than I can bear. I would sooner kill him than see him intimate with you, and where would that leave us? You, a widow, and I, hanging from the gibbet, for murdering a nobleman."

Tears swam in her eyes and she shook her head. "No."

Gavin cupped her face in his hands. "'Tis goodbye we must say, Elizabeth. I must leave your life. Robert is a prince among men. He will care for you and protect you. You will have a good life with him."

He pressed his lips to hers. This kiss would be what he remembered over a lifetime. He swore he would make the most of it.

"Bravo, Gavin," a voice laced with steel said.

22

Elizabeth went rigid. Gavin tore his lips from hers and wheeled. Robert stood in the opening, his shadow lit by the moon behind him. Her nails dug into her palms. This was a nightmare, one she must awaken from. She had to.

"A very touching goodbye, Gavin," Robert added. "I had a feeling you and Elizabeth had grown close."

He turned and gazed at her, a look of pity in his eyes. Robert then focused his attention back upon Gavin.

"You are correct, though, my friend. Kentwood and Fondren are destined to merge. Together, they will make a formidable property. With Elizabeth by my side, 'twill be the premier estate in all southern England."

"'Twill never happen, Robert," Elizabeth hissed. "I'll not allow it."

"You'll not *allow* it?"

She raised her chin a notch. "I shall write to the king myself. I will put an end to this nonsense once and for all."

Robert cocked his head and studied her. Amusement sparkled in his eyes. "And say what, my lady?

You are but a mere woman and at our king's mercy. If he denies my suit and Lord Aldred's request, he will simply marry you off to whomever he chooses. It will be a different life than the one you have grown used to. The one you have led at Kentwood."

He moved a step closer to her. "Be reasonable, Elizabeth. I can give you the world, the lifestyle you desire. Everything you dream of. Gavin can give you nothing. He will hire out as a mercenary, or once the war concludes, he can go out on the tournament circuit. Either way, 'tis no life for you."

"Why do you think he can give me nothing? What gives you that idea?"

Robert smiled sadly at her. "Because he would not choose to go to France otherwise. If he truly loved you, he would petition Edward for your hand in marriage and take you home to live at Ashgrove."

Robert looked over at Gavin. "No, something's amiss with our Sir Gavin. 'Tis obvious some estrangement has occurred betwixt him and his father. Ashgrove is no longer his to possess for some reason. Why else would Ashgrove's heir have settled for being head of Lord Aldred's guard? Any common soldier would suit in that role, not a knight and only son destined to inherit a fortune and great estate."

She looked to Gavin. He remained silent, staring coldly at Robert. She knew he could not deny Robert's words. Her heart rebelled at everything Robert said, but her mind agreed with him.

How could she give up Kentwood? Her people needed her, and she needed them in return. At least Robert was known to her. If he did not seek her hand, King Edward might send her to anywhere in the kingdom. A total stranger would rule every aspect of her life. It would be worse than having lived with her father all those years, for now she knew what true independence was.

She assumed Robert would allow her to maintain the same type of control she had possessed under Aldred.

Or would he?

And far worse, Elizabeth realized, her body would no longer be her own. A stranger would have control of her. After she had experienced making love with Gavin, how could she even think of another man invading her body? Gavin had touched her very soul. She thought of the king forcing her to wed a man years her senior, with few teeth left and a protruding belly, or a man closer to her own age who had a cruel streak. She shivered at the thought of dancing to a new husband's tune.

If she couldn't have Gavin, she might as well take Robert in his stead. Robert was known to her. She could not think him ever being unkind to her. And she would be able to continue her work at Kentwood, she was sure of it. She doubted King Edward would turn down Aldred's request for the match. She must resolve herself to that future.

Gavin sensed the change in Elizabeth. She withdrew into herself, away from him. He had no doubt that given a choice, Elizabeth would cast her lot with Robert, rather than allow King Edward to foist her onto a stranger. Though it cut him to the quick, he knew it best for her.

She turned toward him. Her decision was written plainly across her face. Although he knew it impractical that she would still wish to run away with him, he found it was a bitter thought to swallow.

"No words are necessary, my lady. You do what you must. Women are often forced into situations by the men around them. I hold no animosity toward you."

He swept Elizabeth's hands into his. "I beseech you to know this is right for all involved, my lady." He lifted her hands to his lips and brushed a quick kiss upon her fingers. "I bid you a goodnight and a fond farewell."

He exited the stables, his gait quick. He crossed the bailey, seeing no one.

"Gavin!"

He turned and saw Robert hurrying after him. Robert, the man who would become Elizabeth's husband and lover. 'Twould be better if a knife plunged into his heart than to think of his longtime friend wrapped around Elizabeth's naked curves.

Yet if he could not have what he most desired in this life, Gavin knew he could trust Robert to protect Elizabeth.

He looked at the man who had once been like a brother to him and said, "I know you care for her. I would hope you would continue to give her the independence she is accustomed to. Lord Aldred trusted Elizabeth's judgment. You should do the same."

He took a step toward Robert and thrust out a hand. Robert grasped it in his.

"Love her well, my friend."

It pained Gavin to say these words, but Elizabeth deserved to be loved. He must place her happiness above his own.

Their eyes locked, and Gavin sensed that the camaraderie between them, still a slender thread, survived.

"I will. Trust me on that." Robert tightened the hold on Gavin's hand. They gazed into one another's eyes a moment longer before Gavin stepped away.

"'Twould be most uncomfortable if I stay until the men ship out. I will venture to the coast to find a ship bound for France. I will leave on the morrow."

He turned and strode away, cursing under his breath. The moment he'd heard Robert's voice in the stables, he knew the choice Elizabeth would make. Yet his heart cried out in agony as he walked in solitude to the guardhouse. Didn't she love him for himself alone? Or was it just a castle and the power she wielded within it that she now chose?

Yet he couldn't blame her. He had no land and an unnamed father. What blood coursed through his veins was any man's guess. She couldn't choose him, for he had nothing to offer a lady of her stature. At any rate, the king never would allow their union. Elizabeth was simply being strong for them both. At least this way, one of them would go on. She would continue to rule Kentwood with a firm but just hand.

And he would pray for death to meet him in France. Without Elizabeth at his side, what good would living be?

Elizabeth rose early the next morning. Sleep evaded her throughout the night. Images of Gavin flooded her memory—his smile, his rich laugh, the fire that burned in his eyes when he looked at her. She slammed a fist into her pillow, rage pouring through every pore in her body.

Why must she be a helpless woman? Why couldn't she determine her own destiny?

She dressed with care for mass, hoping to catch a final glimpse of Gavin in the chapel. She matched her smock and kirtle, both of the palest green, with a velvet cotehardie rich as the leaves of the forest's trees. Even her slippers were the same shade as her cotehardie. She brushed her hair until it shone, spilling in waves about her shoulders. She topped it with a circlet of fine gold, a simple band that Gavin once remarked that he liked.

She slipped from her bedchamber and made her way along the stone corridor to the chapel, every step a prayer in her mind. She stood at its door but scanned the place in vain. Gavin must be readying to leave, for no one with his broad shoulders and dark hair was present.

Elizabeth determined she would have one final kiss, one last memory of her soulmate before he left for France. She knew she would never see him again. She feared he would be reckless in battle and take too many risks. She would seek him out, beg him not to go. It would take all the life from her if she thought he rode into battle, taking unnecessary chances with his life. He must want to live. Even if their paths never crossed again, she would be able to sleep at night, knowing he was safe.

She hurried to the stables, hoping she wasn't too late. As she rushed in, she bumped into a stable boy filling a trough with oats.

With a calm she didn't feel, she inquired, "Have you by chance seen Sir Gavin this morning?"

The boy grinned. "Aye, my lady. He left but a few minutes ago. He goes to France to fight for our king." The boy leaned over and picked up something.

Her eyes misted over when she saw Homer in the boy's arms.

"He gave me his cat, that he did. Said he would be a good mouser someday." The boy leaned in and shared a confidence. "Said the beast is spoiled rotten, and I better keep him that way, else Sir Gavin would have my hide when he got back."

Elizabeth realized that although Gavin had told the boy he would return, the words were an empty promise.

She reached out and scratched Homer between his ears, knowing Gavin's fingers had been there at one time. In an instant, she made her decision.

"Saddle my horse. I must get a message to Sir Gavin before he leaves the area."

The child did as told, not questioning her. Elizabeth mounted her horse and raced across the empty yard. Most of Kentwood's residents would be at mass now and break their fast afterward before continuing their tasks.

She reached the gate and signaled the gatekeeper to open the portal. He did so without question. He probably presumed she was off to help in the birth of a child, something she did at odd hours. She waved at him and kicked her heels hard into her steed. Hopefully, she would catch Gavin within the quarter hour if she rode at breakneck speed.

She resolved to ride to the coast itself. She would have her kiss. Damn the consequences. She needed to be in Gavin's arms one more time, taste him, touch him, memorize his face. God's teeth, she would swim to France if she had to, but she would see the love of her life one last time.

Elizabeth rode on as the sun rose in the morning sky. She wondered how hard Gavin must be driving his steed. She was certain she would have caught up with him by this point. Unless he was eager to place a great distance between himself and Kentwood in a short time, that is.

She pushed her horse even harder and was rewarded when she saw a speck in the road ahead. It had to be Gavin. She dug in her heels, and her horse responded with all quickness. As she neared the object, she realized it was two men, neither on horseback.

As she approached, she thought these men might have seen Gavin pass. She would stop and inquire if they had the information she sought.

Both men turned in the road as she drew near. Elizabeth raised a hand to call out a greeting that died in her throat. Neither man was familiar to her, but that was not sufficient cause for alarm. What troubled her was not even their rough dress or unkempt appearance but the fact both men were bound by chains around their wrists and ankles. That meant only one thing.

They were criminals being punished with an eternal pilgrimage. Their sins could be anything from bestiality to incest to murder. They must travel from one holy site to another and hope along the way to gain forgiveness or mercy from some saint. If they did, their chains would be broken. They would regain their freedom to live out their lives how they chose.

Too many criminals sought this kind of punishment, according to Aldred. Because of their great numbers, he often said the roads were becoming unsafe for the average traveler, even those pilgrims who made their own journeys to hallowed places for religious reasons. It was the very reason Aldred insisted she take a guard with her when venturing any length from Kentwood.

She thought it unwise to slow her mount and speak with them. She decided to ride around them and continue her pursuit of Gavin.

As she veered her horse to the left, the man

nearest her stepped directly into her path. Her horse reared and whinnied loudly. She fought for control as his front legs danced in the air. She began to slip from the saddle. As the horse's legs crashed to the ground again, the man grabbed hold of her waist and pulled her from the saddle.

She squirmed as his hands locked tightly around her waist.

"Get the horse!" he called to the other one, who shuffled awkwardly in the lane, his chains hindering his steps. The horse turned and ran in the direction it had come from, back toward Kentwood.

"You simkin!" yelled the man that held her at his companion. "'Zounds, but we could have used that horse. I'm sick and tired of walking mile after mile."

He turned to study her. His fingers bit into her waist as she continued to struggle, pushing her hands against his broad chest. "Aye, but the *morwyn* is a *gwobr*, Owain. And *addien* at that."

Elizabeth frowned at his words. They had a Welsh ring to them, but she knew not what they meant.

The one called Owain tottered over to them. He reached a hand up to stroke her hair, his chains jingling with the movement.

"Ah, *Boneddiges*, Gruffydd simply says that you're a prize, a beautiful prize." He flashed Elizabeth a toothless grin. "We be on a pilgrimage, *Boneddiges*, and have been far too long now."

"'Tis the truth he speaks," agreed Gruffydd. "We've been from one end of Wales to the other and halfway across England now."

"And we haven't come close to finding any pity that 'twould free us from these bonds," added Owain, scratching his chin. "'Course, mayhap we have robbed a traveler or two along the way, but that 'twould not be held against us, I'd think."

The stench that rose from Gruffydd caused a wave of nausea to rise in her. She pushed harder to escape his grasp. He began to laugh at her, his foul breath hot on her cheek. Elizabeth raised both hands and clawed at his cheek with her nails.

Enraged, Gruffydd released her, striking her hard across the face. She fell to her knees, hitting the ground hard, bracing her fall by throwing her hands out flat. The criminal then grabbed a fistful of her hair and raised her head, forcing her to look at him over her shoulder.

"Nay, my pet. Realize we'll have no such nonsense from you, be you a fine lady or not. If we cannot have your horse to ride or sell, we simply have to sell you." He leered at her with malevolence. "You've a pretty face, and mark my words, we are the kind of men to know where to find the right buyer. For you and those fine clothes you wear."

Elizabeth grew faint as his grip tightened, causing her scalp to throb unbearably. Her pale skin burned as he looked down her bodice, smacking his lips as if ready to snack on a favored treat. How dare he think to treat her in such a disrespectful manner? She was mistress of Kentwood. This man was a common offender, marked for all to know him as such. She'd be damned into the fires of Hell itself before she succumbed to him.

Her thoughts raced, but she urged her mind to relax. She must calm herself. She must come up with a plan and quickly.

Before Gruffydd made her life on earth a living hell.

23

"Godspeed to ye, my lord," Old James said as he waved from his doorway. "Rout the French bastards, one and all."

Gavin laughed. "'Twill be mere child's play, Old James. A good day to you."

He mounted his horse and turned it down the lane, glad he'd taken the time to stop and tell the old man goodbye. The lush, green lands of Kentwood lined both sides of the road. As he rode, his eyes shifted to the cottage where only days before, he and Elizabeth made love. The pain of leaving her washed anew over him. He would go mad if he lingered here any longer.

Instead, he must focus on the journey ahead, a brief trip to the coast, a short sea voyage to France, and meeting up with his fellow soldiers from England. He wondered if rumors about his origins had already reached the king. He didn't mind what others thought of him, but it pained him that his mother's reputation would be smeared needlessly.

He regretted not having a more private farewell with Elizabeth, but it would be senseless to prolong their brief interlude. It also might have weakened his resolve to leave immediately for France. Still, he would give his right hand for a ribbon she had worn or a final kiss to savor in his loneliest moments.

A noise ahead caused him to raise his hand to block out the rising sun from his vision. The sound of hooves galloping at this time of morning surprised him. He wondered if a messenger traveled to Kentwood. He still did not know if Lord Aldred had written the promised missive to King Edward that asked if Gavin might be considered for a position in the royal guard. What if this rider brought word from the king?

He determined to flag down the *courlieu* and see what business brought him to Kentwood. Yet as he continued along the road, he spied the horse, riderless, speeding along the thoroughfare. As the horse came in his direction, Gavin recognized it.

It was Elizabeth's horse.

The animal slowed as it approached him, probably recognizing his own mount from the days they'd traveled side by side along this same road. He dismounted and met the horse, speaking to it in soft, gentle tones. The horse came to a complete standstill. He reached up and stroked it, calming the mount.

What was the beast doing out this early, alone, and what had frightened it so?

His stomach lurched uncomfortably. Horses did not saddle themselves. Elizabeth had been astride it at some point up ahead. Whatever terrified the horse caused it to throw her. She could be in the road now, unconscious, bleeding. He must get to her with all haste.

Quickly, he remounted his horse and looped the reins of her horse in his hand. "Come on, fellow. Let's find your mistress." He gave his own horse a swift kick, and both horses set off at a gallop.

Suddenly, a woman's scream tore through the quiet of the morning.

Elizabeth was in trouble.

Gavin dropped the reins of her horse and raced to find her.

———

Elizabeth's scream pierced the air. It surprised Gruffydd so that he released her from his grasp. She raised her skirts and kicked as hard as she could into his groin. The criminal fell to the ground moaning. Without a backward glance at Owain, she dashed away. Surely, she could outrun a man hindered by a set of chains about his ankles. If she were lucky, she would come across her horse and make an even faster escape.

She ignored Owain's loud curses and ran as fast as she dared. She couldn't chance a twisted ankle. If anything slowed her, she feared she wouldn't live long. She looked over her shoulder. Owain's hands danced in the air in balled fists, the thick chain strung between them. His companion still lay crumpled on the ground.

She was safe.

Elizabeth slowed to a trot but kept moving. She looked back over her shoulder twice more and could no longer see the two men. Then she realized she heard a horse coming. She stopped and looked down the road. In the distance she saw a rider. A small piece of her heart wished it could be Gavin, coming to rescue her.

It was Gavin.

Her heart beat wildly in her chest as she recognized him. Lifting her skirts, she began to run toward him.

He rode within ten paces of her and leapt from his horse. He rushed the few feet left between them and threw his arms about her, his mouth crushing hers in a searing kiss. Elizabeth's fingers clung to the front of his tunic. Her knees refused to support her, but Gavin's arms locked about her kept her on her feet.

His kiss was almost punishing, bruising her mouth with its intensity, yet she welcomed it. It let her know she was alive, in Gavin's arms, where she belonged.

He pulled his mouth from hers. They stared wordlessly at each other.

Then he exploded. "What are you doing in the middle of nowhere?" His grip tightened, digging into her shoulders. "Was that your scream? Did your horse throw you? Did—"

"Hush." She placed her fingertips across his mouth. "I was wrong, Gavin. I chose Kentwood over you. I love *you*. *Not* a castle. *Not* a piece of property. I pledge all my love and loyalty *to you*. I will face the king, I will do whatever it takes, but I cannot lose you again, even for a minute." She traced the outline of his mouth with her fingertip. "I refuse to give you up ever again. Let Robert have Kentwood—or let the king do with it as he will. Only tell me you will not leave me again, my love."

Gavin drew her close. She buried her face in his chest. He stroked her hair and along her back. His touch felt so good, so right. How could the king keep them apart when they loved so deeply?

"You ask the impossible, sweetheart." She heard the wistful tone in his voice. "I would give my life for you, but the king will never allow us to wed. We no longer are of the same class. You are far too valuable a prize to squander on a mere foot soldier."

She turned away from him, tears filling her eyes. He was right. Her words of protest died in her throat.

He gasped. "Who struck you?"

She knew he saw the mark Gruffydd put there. The side of her face still burned. It must be swelling. "You said it yourself. My horse threw me. I was on my way to find you."

"No. If you were thrown, you would not have been able to scream to the high heavens. The wind would be knocked from you. I saw you running down the road as if you feared for your life."

He glared at her. "Tell me. What happened?"

She sighed. "It matters not. I took care of it. You need not worry."

Gavin took her chin firmly in his hand. "The truth, Elizabeth. Now. You are hiding something from me."

She swallowed. "I encountered two pilgrims on a penitential. They frightened my horse, and I fell. They scared me a bit, and that is why I screamed and ran away."

He studied her. "You do not tell me the entire story. I see it in your eyes. Come," he said, pulling on her hand. "We shall ride ahead and speak to these men."

He lifted her into the saddle and swung up behind her. His arms went fast about her, and she knew a peace as never before. She leaned against him as he spurred his horse on.

As they sped down the road, she spied her two tormentors. Both were on their feet now, limping along. Her throat tightened at the sight, knowing how close she had come to disaster. Yet Gavin was with her now. Everything would somehow work out. It must.

Owain first spotted them, glancing over his shoulder as they approached. He shouted a curse and hobbled as quickly as he could to escape them. Gruffydd turned and slumped to the ground, his head falling into his hands in defeat.

Gavin rode past Gruffydd and then Owain, turning his horse to block Owain's escape.

"Return to your companion. Now," he commanded.

Owain mumbled under his breath and stalked back to where Gruffydd sat in the road. He turned and shook his fist at Gavin.

"'Twas not me who threatened to sell her, my lord. No, indeed, the thought never crossed my mind."

Gavin jumped from his horse and slipped his hands about Elizabeth's waist, lowering her to the ground. He stormed to where Owain now cowered.

"Sell her? *Sell her?*" he roared.

"Nay. 'Twas Gruffydd who thought to sell her. And her clothes," Owain babbled. "And 'tis he who struck her. Ask the *Boneddiges* herself. 'Twas a perfect gentleman I was, my lord."

Gavin grabbed Owain and tossed him aside as if he weighed less than air. He reached out and yanked Gruffydd to his feet.

"Tell me what you said to her." Gavin's tone was so low and threatening, it brought a chill to Elizabeth. "Tell me now, and I might let you live."

Gruffydd trembled visibly. "Well, 'twas a wild one she is, my lord. Kicked me in me apples, she did. I might never be the same."

Gavin turned to study her. She shrugged. "Aldred told me if I ever found myself in a precarious situation, 'twould be the best thing I could do. He said 'twould be most effective." She grinned sheepishly. "He was right."

Gavin smiled in return. "I would think if they planned to sell you, 'twould be considered dangerous enough to act in such a manner."

His smile fell away as he turned and stared hard at Gruffydd. "You are lucky 'tis all Lady Aldred did to you. And now that I am here, your fate will be far different."

She had no idea what Gavin would do. Beat them senseless? Kill them?

Before she could protest, a muffled sound in the distance distracted them all. She turned and looked far down the road ahead of them. In the distance, dust flew in the road's wake. She saw a large assembly on the move, men marching from the edge of the horizon and beyond.

It was then she saw the banner at the head of the column.

King Edward's retinue was fast approaching.

24

Elizabeth shuddered. The last thing she wanted was a confrontation with England's mercurial monarch in her present state of mind. She did want to speak with King Edward, of course, but she needed time to word her case. The king did not suffer fools. All knew of his famous temper. If he were in a foul mood and she tried to gently coerce him as to a future with Gavin without having thought out every possible angle, she would be destined to fail.

Yet avoiding him was impossible. To be traveling down this road, King Edward had Kentwood as his likely destination.

Her heart caught in her throat. What if he came to pronounce his ruling as to her future? Aldred was hardly cold in his grave. Had the royal already determined to send her to another man, or would he be more amenable to Aldred and Robert's plan for her to remain at Kentwood as Robert's wife?

She looked to Gavin, her throat tight with unshed tears. Gavin was a bastard. He would be among the last of men the king would allow someone of her station to marry. The only acceptable bastards were royal ones.

Gavin seemed to read her mind. He slipped his fingers about hers, entwining them as their bodies had been entwined together. He gave them a gentle squeeze.

"Chin up, my love," he whispered softly. "You wear your emotions on your face today. Do not show Edward how you feel, even when he issues his command for you."

He lifted her hand to his cheek and rested it there a moment. He closed his eyes briefly, as if he savored her very touch, before brushing a kiss across her knuckles. "Be strong, my lady," he said, looking into her eyes. "You are known for your control and keen intelligence. Live up to King Edward's expectations."

Gavin released her hand. As it dropped to her side, a searing loneliness penetrated Elizabeth to her core. How could she live in a world without the only man she would ever love?

She blinked back the tears that threatened to fall and steeled herself for the encounter with her king. She must be on her toes at all times. Edward was a wily one. She could not let her guard fall for a moment.

And sometime before he left Kentwood, she would persuade him to allow her to marry Gavin. She hadn't the vaguest notion how to accomplish that goal, the most important in her life. She would, though.

Because she was Elizabeth of Kentwood.

A rider from the distant entourage approached them. Gavin looked to the two pilgrims.

"Out of the way. Stand by the side of the road.

And not a word from you." He glared at Gruffydd, in particular.

The two figures shuffled to the edge of the lane, an air of submission about them.

Edward's rider arrived and quickly dismounted. "Be ye Lady Aldred of Kentwood?" he asked hesitantly.

"I am."

Pride swelled within Gavin. Despite the bruise on her cheek, Elizabeth stood tall now, her emotions masked from the world. She looked as regal as any queen. Her bearing suddenly gave him pause. She was now a widow. What if Edward himself came for her? What if the English monarch wanted Elizabeth in his bed? Gavin had heard tales of how the king was taken with her.

He forced the idea aside. He couldn't let unfounded jealousy be the cause of him murdering England's king.

"King Edward comes to pay you a visit, my lady." The young messenger frowned. "He did expect you to be at Kentwood, though."

She sent a harsh look at the thin rider. "I have an estate to run, young man. If I am out and about, 'tis business I see to and no concern of yours."

The rider blushed. "Beg pardon, my lady. Would you care for me to ride on to Kentwood and announce the king's imminent arrival, or would you care to do so?"

Elizabeth replied, "I shall return to Kentwood. I would choose to meet my king in more appropriate attire."

She glanced over at the two fugitives. "Would you have Edward's steward deal with these men? 'Tis Kentwood they have come to, and we have no shrine here for them to grovel at and beg mercy. I wish them gone from my lands."

"Of course, my lady. They will trouble you no further. I shall stay with them until the king's retinue arrives and hand them over." The messenger glanced over his shoulder. "I would say you have slightly more than half of an hour before his majesty arrives at Kentwood."

"Then I shall make haste."

She turned to him. Gavin realized they had only the one horse between them. Elizabeth's horse must still be down the road a ways.

"Let me assist you into the saddle, my lady," Gavin said. "You may ride back to Kentwood. I shall locate the other horse and return upon it."

"No. I require your presence at Kentwood, my lord. Please accompany me there now."

Gavin did want to speak to King Edward about his future at some point. It might be easier to do so from Kentwood when the king was well rested and fed, rather than accosting him in the middle of a dusty country road.

"As you wish." He stepped to his horse as she followed him. He placed her into the saddle and swung up behind her, taking the reins and spurring the horse on.

As they rode, Gavin savored holding Elizabeth close to him one last time. Her auburn curls gleamed in the sunlight. He couldn't resist stroking them.

Her hand caught his. She turned and kissed the open palm. Fire roared in his belly. How could he give up this woman, whose touch, whose kiss took him to heights as never before? He raged inwardly at the unfairness of a society which kept lovers apart.

He spied her wayward horse ahead of them. He

slowed his own to a trot and then pulled up alongside the other beast. He removed himself from the saddle and looked up. Elizabeth's beauty was heartbreaking. It caused his mouth to go dry.

Swallowing hard, he said, "You should return upon your own mount. Let us hurry. 'Tis much you have to do to try and prepare before the king's retinue arrives."

Gavin reached for her, his hands easily spanning her waist, and took her from the saddle. She planted her hands firmly on his shoulders even as she pressed her lips to his in a fervent kiss.

He needed no more invitation. This would be their kiss to remember for all time. They would never again find themselves isolated from all others as they did now. Gavin let her slide down his body and held her close. He kissed her with every ounce of love he held for her, every bit of passion she had stirred within him, as deeply and completely a kiss as a man had ever given to a woman. His hands pushed through her tangled curls as he sought to remember her taste, the velvet softness of her mouth, the feel of her breasts against his chest.

Then he broke the kiss. "I would go on and on, my love, but we have not the time. I doubt there would ever be enough time for me to convey the depths of my love for you." He swept her hands into his and brought them to his lips for a last, ardent kiss.

"As the sun rises every day, know that my love for you rises within me until the end of all time."

Before she could speak, Gavin set her into her saddle and quickly reclaimed his own mount. Without a glance in Elizabeth's direction, he kicked his heels. The horse took off. He heard her horse follow.

As they came to the crossroads that turned off toward Fondren, Gavin spied Robert riding in their direction. He slowed his horse as they approached. Elizabeth pulled up behind him.

Robert called out a greeting as he quizzically looked at them. "A good morn to you both. Are you all right, Elizabeth?" he asked. "Your cheek is quite bruised."

"Lady Elizabeth had a mishap with her horse," Gavin replied. "She is returning to Kentwood to prepare for the king's arrival."

Robert nodded. "So I gathered." He hesitated a moment and then said, "The king sent a rider to Fondren, requesting me to meet him at Kentwood."

Elizabeth spoke up. "Please excuse me. I must alert my servants that the king comes and change my attire." She rode off without waiting for their reply.

Robert watched her leave and then looked back at him. "So, Gavin, I thought you left for France this morning. Did Elizabeth feel the need to accompany you to the coast?"

He ignored the tinge of sarcasm in his friend's voice and replied, "I was on the road when I ran into the king's messenger. I decided to return. I would ask Edward about my request to serve in his royal guard since I had no word in that respect. If not, I will ask to join with the troops now with him. Surely after he completes his business at Kentwood, they will be off for the coast and the wars in France."

Robert nodded. "A wise choice, my friend." He placed a hand on Gavin's shoulder. "I would not have us part on ill terms. I wish you the best of luck in France, whatever capacity you will serve in."

Robert turned his horse in the direction of Kentwood. Gavin sighed. The minute he had spied Robert, he knew King Edward had sent for him. 'Twould be only a matter of time before the monarch announced Robert's betrothal to Elizabeth.

Gavin's horse followed, but his heart was heavy as he returned to Kentwood. It seemed as if he rode to his own execution.

25

Elizabeth smoothed her sideless surcoat, a deep gold silk embroidered with slashes of hunter green. Her kirtle was the same shade of green. Nelia had fussed over her swollen cheek, heating a stone in the fire and then tossing it into a basin of water. Elizabeth had bathed the bruise in this water while two other servants removed her soiled clothing and redressed her in finery fit to receive a king.

Nelia also insisted that her hair be up, coiled around her ears and head and covered with a golden caul. She proclaimed Elizabeth a young girl no longer. She should greet her king with more than a simple circlet about her wild array of curls. It felt strange to wear the thick, heavy silk netting over her hair since she rarely did so.

Still, she wanted to look her best for the sovereign. He was meticulous about his own dress, and she wished to mirror him in that respect.

She looked out over the bailey. Gavin had changed into a gray cotehardie, etched in silver along its neck and sleeves. He stood at the head of the guard next to Rufus, his hair combed, shining like midnight in the sunshine. She caught Rufus's eye and inclined her head to him. She knew it was Rufus that had insisted Gavin stand with him, as the captain of the guard, even though Gavin had relinquished his position as of last night.

The royal retinue streamed into the courtyard now, at least fifty horsemen accompanying an ornate litter. The king rode next to the litter on a destrier black as ink. Elizabeth's curiosity rose a notch. Who accompanied King Edward? The queen rarely left the royal palace. Surely, he had not brought his mistress to Kentwood?

She descended the steps as the royal monarch dismounted. He tossed his reins to a retainer and stepped toward her. As always, first sight of the king caused her heart to flutter in nervous anticipation. The first time he'd called at Kentwood, her belly roiled for days before the appointed visit. Aldred had laughed heartily at her misery, telling her to relax.

"He's only a man, my dearest, and often out of sorts, much as a bad-tempered child."

True, Edward's famous temper came and went as fast as lightning flashed in the sky. When he was in a good mood, he was most impressive. Tall, regal, with a smile just this side of wicked, England's king was always a man to be reckoned with.

Elizabeth curtseyed low as he approached, tamping down her nerves. Too much lay on the line for her to act as a simpering girl. She must impress this king, entertain him, and cajole him into the best of humors if she were to work up the courage to make her unorthodox request.

"Up, up, my lady," he commanded. He took her hand and appraised her thoroughly. She wondered if he would comment upon her swollen cheek. "Fit to receive a king, you are, Lady Aldred, and what a splendid cotehardie. But why have you muzzled that glorious hair of yours?"

Edward frowned, always the first sign his temper could shift.

"I am getting on in years, sire. I thought it more appropriate to wear it up as a woman of my age should."

He snorted. "I bloody well won't have much beauty to look upon in France, my lady. Seeing your glorious mane of hair was but one of my reasons for even coming Kentwood way."

She smoothly replied, "Then I will make haste to please Your Majesty." She removed the caul from her head, pins scattering everywhere, and shook out her hair with her fingers. It cascaded down her back.

Edward smiled, mollified for the moment. "Much better, my lady. Now if you will only tell me you have some of those pear tarts for me, all will be forgiven."

She returned his smile. "Pear and plum, sire. I thought it wise for you to have some of each." She breathed an inner sigh of relief, knowing the tarts to be in the ovens as they spoke. Having entertained the king before, the Kentwood kitchens knew the royal's likes and dislikes. She prayed they would be ready in time to satisfy his hunger pangs for them.

He linked his arm through hers. "Now that's the Kentwood spirit." He led her over to the litter and motioned for servants to draw aside the curtains.

"I would like to introduce you to someone, my lady."

Elizabeth watched as a velvet-slippered foot emerged, followed by a cotehardie of peacock blue. A young woman of about a score-and-two stepped from the litter. She, too, wore her hair loose about her shoulders, a silver circlet its only adornment. The woman raised hesitant eyes to hers.

"May I present Anne, widow of Lord Addleby? 'Tis Elizabeth, widow of Lord Aldred that you now see."

Lady Addleby dropped a curtsy to Elizabeth, who returned the favor. "'Tis so kind of you to receive me, Lady Aldred," she said softly.

Elizabeth admired her new guest's perfect, alabaster skin and eyes that were as green as Elizabeth's own, as well as her bashful smile.

But what was she doing here at Kentwood?

"The king said you are a widow, as am I. I am sorry for your loss. 'Tis it a recent one?" she asked.

Lady Addleby shook her head. "No, I lost Lord Addleby nigh on two years ago." A frown crossed her face, and Elizabeth decided to pry no further.

"Then shall we go in, Your Highness?" She looked around. "I do not see many of your men present. I thought there was quite a mass headed toward Kentwood."

King Edward waved a hand in the air. "These are the necessary servants and a few of my commanders. The rest of the men will camp outside Kentwood's walls. You are under no obligation to feed them, my lady. They may fend for themselves."

She knew exactly what that meant. Though she'd had no notice of Edward's visit, he would expect her to feed his entire retinue, and well. If not, he would be in a surly mood, and the army encamped outside Kentwood's walls would wreak havoc upon her tenants.

"Nay, sire. We have more than enough to accommodate all your men, even a thousand more, should they show up."

His eyes gleamed at her remarks. She breathed a

sigh of relief. Already, the kitchens were busy preparing the mid-day meal in addition to the fruit tarts, and it would truly be a feast fit for a king. The men working in the Kentwood fields would have to wait their turn, but she would send word to them of what to expect if they exercised patience.

"Then let us adjourn inside. The sun already grows hot." Edward looked around and spotted Robert.

"Sir Robert? 'Tis you?"

Robert scurried over and bowed. "Greetings, Your Majesty. I received your message and came in all due haste."

King Edward nodded. "And what of Sir Gavin? I received word that he resides at Kentwood these days." He looked around again and snapped his fingers.

Elizabeth motioned for Gavin to join them. He strode over and knelt before the king.

"Oh, by the Virgin, rise off your feet, boy. Come with us." Edward nodded to Robert. "See Lady Addleby inside the keep."

As the king took Elizabeth's arm and started up the steps, she resisted the urge to glance over her shoulder at Gavin. She wondered if King Edward would speak to Gavin about the missive Aldred wrote in his behalf.

"I shall nap for two hours' time," Edward announced to her as they made their way inside the castle. "I fear I slept poorly last night. Then we shall dine and mayhap hunt the remainder of the afternoon. Kentwood always had ample deer and elk, if I remember correctly."

"Let me escort you to your room, Your Majesty,"

she replied, grateful for the additional time the king's nap would give her servants.

He frowned. "No, let Sir Gavin see me up. I wish to speak to him on an important matter."

Elizabeth moved away and curtseyed. Gavin stepped up and took her place. She mouthed *solar* to him, and Gavin ushered the king away.

She turned back to her unexpected guest. "Come, Lady Addleby. Sir Robert will keep you company for me. I fear I have a few things to supervise before we can settle down for our midday meal."

Lady Addleby's laughter tinkled softly. "Oh, my lady, you handle him so beautifully." Her gaze met Elizabeth's. "He simply frightens me to death. But you, you look directly at him and speak with such self-assurance."

Robert laughed. "Elizabeth is famous for being self-assured. If a dragon roared into the great hall now, she would stomp her foot and order it away as an uninvited guest."

Lady Addleby looked to Robert, her eyes wide. "And what if this dragon did not wish to go?"

He grinned. "Then Elizabeth would pull a sword from the closest man's sheath and whack it into tiny pieces." He glanced toward her. "Of course, she'd complain about the mess it made before she had Cook turn it into some delicious stew."

She felt her cheeks heat. Robert seemed the Robert of old, not the stranger who had taken his place in recent days. She prayed his good mood did not hinge on his belief that King Edward arrived at Kentwood to give Elizabeth to him in marriage. She had enough to worry about at the moment.

Instead, she pushed her fears away. "Sir Robert will keep you entertained, my lady. Simply ignore most of what he says and indulge him with a few meaningless compliments. He loves to tell war stories of his time in France. If you become too bored, do not fear. I shall be close by to rescue you."

The young noblewoman smiled graciously. "I feel that I am in capable hands, Lady Aldred." She looked up at Robert and blushed.

Elizabeth walked away. Nelia joined her as she exited the great hall.

"Everything under control?" she asked.

The servant nodded. "He has surprised us before, the old bugger. We will handle things."

"Nelia!" Elizabeth reprimanded. "He is our king."

She snorted. "King or no, he will not catch Kentwood unprepared." The servant stalked off, her head held high with pride.

Elizabeth continued up the stairs and down the hall toward the solar. She wasn't about to let King Edward speak to Gavin and not know what was being said. A little eavesdropping was sometimes a necessary measure that every woman had to take.

26

As they entered the solar, Gavin noticed immediately that food and wine stood upon a table. He admired Elizabeth for thinking ahead in every area. He had no doubt that the meal served to the king would consist of the choicest delicacies. Although she'd had no notice of the king's impending arrival, the mistress of Kentwood always thought fast on her feet.

King Edward breezed in as if he owned the solar and spent every day within its walls. He fell into a chair next to the window, one of Aldred's little luxuries. The royal gazed out the glass, lost in thought a moment.

"Pour me some wine," he finally ordered. "And bring me that bowl of fruit."

He did as requested and retreated a few steps.

"No, no, no. Come and sit across from me, Sir Gavin. We must talk of important matters."

Moving closer, he waited for King Edward to initiate the conversation. The monarch dawdled, first inspecting one piece of fruit at a time before finally selecting an apple to munch upon. He sipped his wine slowly and would stop and swirl it in the glass before taking another drink.

Gavin thought time stood still. He was anxious to hear the king's words, but Edward seemed in no mood to be rushed. Gavin, never the most patient of men, locked his jaw tightly to keep from blurting out for the monarch to get on with things.

Finally, the king lost interest in his food and drink and pushed them both aside. He gazed at Gavin thoughtfully.

"What is it like, those French prisons? Are they as atrocious as ours?"

Gavin flinched inwardly. Memories of pain after harsh punishments, bitter loneliness, and over-whelming sadness flooded him. He steeled himself against the raging emotions that warred within him and took a calming breath before he answered.

"The first place I was held was but a small room with a few pieces of simple furniture, sire. No enter-tainment of any kind except a chess set in which to pass the long days, waiting for word from home."

Edward's eyes gleamed at him. "But you had Sir Robert with you then, did you not?"

He nodded. "Yes. I might have lost my reason had I not had Robert to talk with."

"But then your good friend was ransomed."

Gavin's hands fisted. He forced himself to released his fingers and remain calm. "Yes, sire."

"And you were not."

He wondered just how much Edward knew. It was said the king liked to toy with his subjects. Gavin began to feel like one of Edward's playthings

"No. My father, Lord Ashton, did not authorize release of the monies requested."

Gavin's chest swelled tightly. He found it hard to

breathe. He had tried to forget about Berwyn's cruel actions, but he realized now he never would.

"The bastards moved you to another place?"

"Yes," he responded woodenly. "'Twas a true prison. A large cell. Many, many prisoners crammed within it. I cannot begin to describe to you the filth present there."

Edward chuckled. "We all know the French to be a dirty lot, do we not, Sir Gavin?"

He felt his king tried to lighten the mood some, so he only nodded, his eyes downcast.

"I know the reason why Lord Ashton disowned you."

Edward's voice was now quiet. Gavin raised his eyes and saw the sympathetic look the monarch wore.

"He wrote to me as soon as he learned of Gillian's... *indiscretion*. He wanted it made known that you were no son of his." Edward leaned forward in his seat. "I am sorry for that, Sir Gavin. One of you is worth tenfold of Lord Ashton. To think you will not inherit Ashgrove is criminal."

"I do not deserve it, my king, nor would I seek a claim to it," he replied fiercely. "My eyes are turned toward other goals now."

"Yes, yes," Edward murmured. "Lord Aldred wrote me of such things."

"I was not certain he had done so. We discussed the matter shortly before his passing. I did not know if he had time to write the missive because of his ill health."

"Oh, yes. He did. Aldred always wrote to me of a great many things."

Edward's eyes shone with some hidden knowledge. Gavin was not certain what the king was up to, but he could only play along in his game.

"Did you like Lady Addleby?" Edward asked suddenly. "She is a rare prize. Almost as rare as Lady Aldred."

Gavin thought no women held a candle to his Elizabeth, but he would not insult his king with a churlish observation.

"She is very beautiful indeed, sire."

"She is widowed now. Would you care to wed her?"

Edward's words took him aback. He did not want to offend the sovereign, but he could not see himself with any other woman but Elizabeth. Yet how could he avoid the mess now before him? Edward would only have brought up the matter because he wanted to see a union between the pair.

"Sire, she is indeed lovely, but I have no home to offer her. My place is now that of a commoner, on the front lines of battle. The Black Prince himself will vouch for my steadfastness in war. I would only wish to fight for England or serve you in your royal guard. I have no wish for a wife."

"None? None whatsoever?" Edward scratched his chin thoughtfully. "And I thought I had a free estate in the west that I could settle upon you."

Suddenly, Elizabeth burst through the room from behind a dressing panel. Gavin saw her flushed face and realized she had overheard Edward's offer to him. He didn't venture to guess how she'd gotten there in the first place.

"Forgive me for barging in, sire," she said, out of breath. "I could not help but overhear your words to Sir Gavin."

Gavin's eyes quickly cut to see how Edward

would react to such a statement. To eavesdrop on the king was unthinkable. Elizabeth might very well be signing her own death warrant with such an admission. Instead of anger, however, he caught a glimmer of amusement in the king's eyes. Gavin glanced back at Elizabeth.

She gazed at Edward, her chin held high, as she waited for Edward to grant her permission to speak. The king nodded, and Elizabeth turned and looked at Gavin briefly before she began.

"Sir Gavin would make a fine owner of this estate you mention, Your Majesty. He picks up on the smallest of details and has made many intelligent suggestions that have helped me in running Kentwood since my husband's passing."

Her words shocked Gavin. Why was she pushing him into the arms of another woman, unless she wanted him kept away from the war?

Before he could protest, she continued. "I also have a suggestion of my own to make, begging your pardon. I would wish to be allowed to enter Queen Philippa's service. Or I could serve in another capacity in one of the royal households. I would wish to——"

"You certainly are demanding, Lady Aldred." Edward steepled his fingers and regarded her with a solemn expression. "I had other plans for you."

She dropped to her knees in front of Edward. "I know those plans, Sire. Robert confessed of his and Aldred's schemes. I know you came to tell me that I must marry Robert and join our estates together."

"Indeed? So these are my plans for you, my lady?"

Her face now betrayed her turmoil. "Oh, Your Majesty, Sir Robert is a fine man, finer than many in the kingdom, but he is not for me."

She looked to Gavin. Their eyes locked. His heart

pounded as she said, "I love Sir Gavin, Your Highness. I love him with all my being and cannot even look upon another. I realize I am a political pawn, but please, please, for Aldred's sake and the good service he gave to you, let me marry no man. I appeal to your sense of fairness and wisdom, my king. Please show mercy to me and give the estate of which you speak to Sir Gavin."

Edward studied Elizabeth. Gavin longed to reach out and touch her, stop her trembling, but he was frozen in place.

"You say you want no man, or none other than Sir Gavin." He tilted his head as he looked at her. "Then would you even enter a nunnery if I asked it of you? And remember," he cautioned, "I know of your wild ways as a child."

Tears began to course down Elizabeth's cheeks. She bowed her head and responded, "I would do so most willingly, sire. I love Sir Gavin that much. Whatever you ask, I will comply."

Gavin could no longer stay silent and leaped to his feet. "I will not let you do that, Elizabeth! You can't throw your life away." He crossed the room and knelt beside her, taking her hands in his.

"Sweetheart, don't be a fool. You can keep Kentwood. Make Lord Aldred proud. Keep your people happy. Please, my dearest, marry Robert. He loves you. I shall go to France. You will soon forget me. I promise."

She smiled sadly through her tears. "Forget you? How can I forget the face that I dream of every night, the one I long to glimpse each minute of every day? You think going to France and deliberately putting yourself in harm's way until you are killed will make me happy? No, Gavin. My people would never be happy if I am not. The king must find an heir that will satisfy them and keep Kentwood thriving."

She pulled her hands from his and faced their sovereign again. "I apologize profusely for my bold words, sire, and beg of you to give me leave. Only protect Gavin. Don't let him go back to France. He has suffered enough." She rose. "I will leave you now. I apologize for my intrusion."

Edward held a hand out. "No, my lady. Stay. I have this situation firmly in hand. I will simply name Sir Gavin heir to Kentwood. After all, he is Aldred's son, and it was Aldred's deathbed wish for his son to inherit his estate."

The king's words stunned Gavin. He stumbled to his feet.

Aldred's son? He was Aldred's son

A shock of disbelief ran through him. Yet even as the words lingered in his mind, he knew them to be true. Aldred, a father truer to him than Berwyn ever had been, a warrior and gentleman like no other could ever be, had been his very sire.

A wave of desolation hit Gavin. Aldred was now lost to him. Had his father always known of their relationship? He pushed the thought aside. He would not allow bittersweet regret to rule his life. Simply knowing Aldred had been his father was enough. A sense of relief settled over him, a happiness that the mystery of his bloodline was solved.

He looked to Elizabeth. She'd gone stark white, the color drained from her face.

He pulled her to her feet. "Are you all right, sweetheart?" He cradled her cheek in his hand.

"Yes," she answered him. "Just dazed. Why would my lord husband never have mentioned such a thing?"

King Edward chuckled. "Aldred only realized the truth when Sir Gavin arrived a few weeks past. When he heard what had occurred to Sir Gavin when he returned to Ashgrove after escaping from prison, Aldred wrote to me immediately."

Gavin turned to Edward as the king spoke. "Lady Ashton had not told Aldred of the child they made just before she wed Lord Ashton. More than likely, she herself did not know. 'Twas only after Aldred heard what Lord Ashton had done that Aldred realized Gavin must be his son."

Edward smiled indulgently. "After all, there is a passing resemblance between them. In any case, Aldred wrote me and conveyed all this news shortly before he died."

The king paused and downed the remainder of his wine. "He also wanted his widow to marry *you*, my lord. Not Sir Robert as he had previously requested."

Gavin's heart nearly burst from happiness at the king's words. He slipped Elizabeth's hand into his, hoping it was no dream.

Then he remembered Edward's words from a few minutes before and frowned. "What of your offer for me to wed Lady Addleby and settle in the west?"

The king shrugged, a mischievous smile tugging at the corners of his mouth. "Mayhap I thought to tempt you a bit. She is a sweet morsel. Nay," he continued. "I brought along the girl as a bride for Sir Robert. Hopefully, she will appease him, for he will be losing out on marriage to Lady Aldred."

"Then, we *are* to wed?" Elizabeth asked, wonder in her voice.

"Yes, of course," Edward said benignly. "The

sooner, the better. Unless you would like to enter that convent, after all."

"Nay!" she cried. "I have found my bit of heaven on earth right here, with the man I will love until my dying day and even beyond the grave."

Gavin felt the tears on his own cheeks as he enveloped Elizabeth within the circle of his arms.

"Elizabeth, will you do me the honor of becoming my wife?" he asked formally.

Her face radiated love, and he caught the desire that began to light her eyes. "Yes, Gavin, son of Aldred and Gillian. My dreams will come to pass with our marriage."

Gavin lowered his mouth to hers in a hungry kiss as Edward's loud laughter rang throughout the solar.

EPILOGUE
KENTWOOD—1367

The troubadour finished his song. All present in the great hall of Kentwood applauded the musician's efforts. Elizabeth looked over at Anne, who was heavy with child.

"Are you comfortable, my dear?" Robert asked his wife. "Would you care for a little more of the mulled wine?"

"That would be lovely. And please go and find me another one of those apple tarts. You know how my sweet tooth grows at these times."

Robert kissed his wife's fingers. "Come, Gavin, we're on a mission of mercy and cannot return until we have succeeded in locating a score of apple tarts."

Gavin laughed and stood. "Anything for you, my love?" he asked Elizabeth, a smile on his face.

"No. Unless you wish to save Rufus from Aldred's pestering questions and the troubadour's lute from Joan's fierce plucking. And little Gillian looks tired. Would you ask Nelia to put her to bed?"

He grinned. "Anything else, my commander?"

She blushed at her husband's teasing. "No, be off with you. But do see to all the children."

As the two men left, Anne remarked, "You really are like a general, Elizabeth. Always ordering people about." She smiled saucily. "Even your dearest companions."

She patted her friend's hand. "Now if only I could order your babe to come. 'Tis well time when you should deliver, you know."

"Oh, Elizabeth, you cannot control everything."

She beamed. "But I can try, Anne. I can always try." She ran her fingers through Homer's silky coat. The cat purred contentedly in Elizabeth's lap as the women chatted.

Soon, Robert returned with two of the apple tarts for his wife. Elizabeth was pleased that his marriage to Anne had been a successful one. It seemed they were smitten with each other at first sight the day Anne arrived at Kentwood with the king, all those years ago. She sighed, happy that their friendships had survived the events of the past.

Her husband returned, a somber look on his face.

"Which child is it, Gavin? You never look so serious unless one of the children ails," she said.

He shook his head. "No, all our brats are fine. Unless you count a broken string on the troubadour's lute."

"That Joan for you. She is a handful."

He lifted a lock of her hair. "Just like you were at her age, my pet."

"Oh, Gavin, you didn't even know me then."

He smiled. "I know. But there are stories, I hear."

He looked over to Robert and Anne. "Something has come up that requires our attention, though. Would you excuse us?"

Gavin reached down and removed Homer from

Elizabeth's lap, setting the cat on the floor. He stretched lazily and wandered off in search of new attention. Gavin took her hand and pulled her to her feet. He escorted her out of the great hall and down to a small alcove in the stone corridor. He drew her into it and caught her up in his arms.

"So this is what requires our attention, my lord? Oh, sir, 'tis very dark in here," she teased. "I might not be able to follow your conversation."

He held her fast. "Then I must let you lead, and I will follow."

Elizabeth took his face in her hands and pulled his mouth down to hers. The minute their lips touched, it was as if sparks ignited. That liquid fire that always seemed to burn in her belly at Gavin's touch began to flame, and she lost herself in her husband's passionate kiss.

Some minutes later, he lifted his mouth from hers.

"I just had to touch you," he said. He brushed his lips tenderly over hers. "I thank the stars every day for Lord Aldred. Our marriage would never have come to pass had it not been at his request."

"He did bring us together," she whispered, running her fingers along his jaw. "He and King Edward made everything possible. For you to own Kentwood and regain your good name."

"For me to have *you*," he said. He kissed her again, a long, lingering kiss, full of promise. "I would care for none of this without you, my love."

Elizabeth smiled. "Then mayhap we should go work on making another babe, my lord. If 'tis a boy, we could name it after King Edward since we already have an Aldred."

Gavin's low laugh sounded near her ear. "You are a most intelligent woman, Elizabeth mine. Lucky was the day I wed you."

And with that, his mouth came down on hers again.

ALSO BY ALEXA ASTON

THE HOLLYWOOD NAME GAME

Hollywood Heartbreaker

Hollywood Flirt

Hollywood Player

Hollywood Double

Hollywood Enigma

Lawmen of the West

Runaway Hearts

Blind Faith

Love and the Lawman

Ballad Beauty

DUKES OF DISTINCTION:

Duke of Renown

Duke of Charm

Duke of Disrepute

Duke of Arrogance

Duke of Honor

MEDIEVAL RUNAWAY WIVES:

Song of the Heart

A Promise of Tomorrow

Destined for Love

SOLDIERS AND SOULMATES:

To Heal an Earl

To Tame a Rogue

To Trust a Duke

To Save a Love

To Win a Widow

THE ST. CLAIRS:

Devoted to the Duke

Midnight with the Marquess

Embracing the Earl

Defending the Duke

Suddenly a St. Clair

THE KING'S COUSINS:

God of the Seas

The Pawn

The Heir

The Bastard

THE KNIGHTS OF HONOR:

Rise of de Wolfe

Word of Honor

Marked by Honor

Code of Honor

Journey to Honor

Heart of Honor

Bold in Honor

Love and Honor

Gift of Honor

Path to Honor

ABOUT THE AUTHOR

A native Texan and former history teacher, award-winning and internationally bestselling author Alexa Aston lives with her husband in a Dallas suburb, where she eats her fair share of dark chocolate and plots out stories while she walks every morning. She enjoys travel, sports, and binge-watching—and never misses an episode of *Survivor*.

Alexa brings her characters to life in steamy historicals, contemporary romances, and romantic suspense novels that resonate with passion, intensity, and heart.

KEEP UP WITH ALEXA
Visit her website
Newsletter Sign-Up

MORE WAYS TO CONNECT WITH ALEXA

CPSIA information can be obtained
at www.ICGtesting.com
Printed in the USA
LVHW041328060222
710388LV00011B/1733